PRIDE

Robert Santoro

author**HOUSE**®

AuthorHouse™
1663 Liberty Drive
Bloomington, IN 47403
www.authorhouse.com
Phone: 1-800-839-8640

First published by AuthorHouse   01/05/2012
Cover artwork is an imprint of SterlingHouse Publisher, Inc.

ISBN: 978-1-4685-2546-5 (sc)
ISBN: 978-1-4685-2545-8 (ebk)

Printed in the United States of America

Dedication

This book is dedicated to the bravest two boys anyone could ever have the privilege of meeting—my 10 year old twin sons, Jake and Chase.

You are the single best team in the world . . . one, a "Warrior", the other, a "Hero". Together, you fought back hard, gave cancer a well-deserved kick in the ass, stood beside each other and as brothers, you tamed the giant. DONE!

I am proud to call myself your dad . . .

Day: minus seven (-7)—a letter to my son Posted Oct 14, 2010 9:27pm October 14, 2010

To my son, Jake,

I know at the moment you are far too sick to read this or even have mommy read this to you but when you are better (and I promise you we WILL get you better) I will read you this letter so that you will know exactly how I feel about you as my little boy and how amazed I am at how you have conducted yourself over the past 100 days—as a father, I want you to know that I could not be prouder of you. Never, no way, not ever!

No father could be prouder; not the father of the US Marine who just won the Medal of Honor for saving his entire battalion, or the dad whose boy was just accepted to Harvard on full academic scholarship, or the guy whose kid scored the winning touchdown and was carried off the field by his teammates, or even the old man whose son just won the Nobel Peace Prize. In my book you top all of these men—and you are just a little boy. TRUTH!

You and I have not really spoken in a while, or at least we have not spoken as we once did, like on "special days" we would share together, or when we skated together, or when I would read to you before bedtime, but I have tried to tell you, and I am not sure you fully comprehend me at this time, that I love you more than words can express. I do. I love you with all of my heart and if there was anything I could do at all to change places with you it would have been done before they even picked you up from school the day you were diagnosed with this horrible disease—I promise you that! in a second i would be in that bed in your place if i could!

I want you to know that there is nothing mommy, Chase and I haven't done and will not do to try to make you feel comfortable and feel more secure—We ALL love you so,so much and our lives are on hold until you come home—for as long as it takes, and that includes Kaos, that is a promise.

I know that the summer passed by and now the leaves are changing colors and school stared. But do you know what? No one swam in the pool because it was no fun without you, football and ice hockey did not have winning seasons like when you and Chase were on the teams and we have not let Chase step foot in Austin Road even though school started over a month ago. Perhaps illegal, but who cares!

On the 4th of July I watched TV alone at the house and never once looked up at the sky, on Halloween I am putting a sign on the door that says "come back next year for 2 Kit Kats" on Thanksgiving I am fasting and on your birthday I will bring the best cake for you and your brother to Memorial that you have ever seen!

BUT THEN THERE IS CHRISTMAS! We WILL have you home for Christmas and can you even imagine what Santa is going to do for a brave little Warrior like you and a Hero like Chase? We will need to put on an extension to the house for all of the toys!! Are you ready for that?

So maybe the summer passed and the leaves have changed colors but I want you to know this, Chase, mom and I will wait until the end of time for you and we will never move on without you! EVER! We are a family and that is all!

Unfortunately, there is some stupid law that sais Chase has to eventually get to school and perhaps after transplant he will. But, he is your biggest fan, your lifelong friend, your one-minute younger twin brother and our HERO. He is only going back to Austin Road to keep your "crew" in line until you get there and to let them all know how tough Jake the Snake really is. Tough as nails!

You and Chase are the bravest boys (and perhaps men) on the planet. Everyone in town, and I mean everyone, knows about you and thinks you are an absolute Rock Star. You are a Warrior in every sense and you and Chase have become an absolute inspiration to me and mom and an entire community. You are role models to all and you are not even 9 years old. I have no words to express how this makes me feel.

Please know you WILL get better, we WILL once again have special days and you will score another hat trick (don't think I forgot that day because I haven't and never will!—i still have the puck in my office) we will go on family vacations again, play on our zip line, swim in our pool, play sports and we will explore this world together as a family—that I promise you!

I love you with all of my heart and when you are better, you Chase and I will do great things to rid this world of this horrible disease. If anyone can make that happen, we can!

Be strong my little Warrior and FIGHT as hard as you can—punch, scream, bite and kick if you have to! Fight dirty because this disease sure does. But know this, i will be right there beside you punching, screaming, biting and kicking as well. But you know what—you are beating it—you are winning just like you always have in the past! Day zero is only seven more days away and then our HERO your brother, Chase the Ace is on his way for the Jake Chase ONE-TWO COMBO. PUNCH!.

You are the best team in the world and nothing can beat the two of you together. I know that, and, as your dad, I have seen it many, many times in everything you boys have done together!

I miss you more than I can possibly can ever begin express on this page. You are my inspiration, and what dad says that to his 9 year old?

All the love to you that this world and I can offer,

Dad

As I promised my son, we will now do great things to rid this world of this horrible disease. Accordingly, a portion of every book I sell will be donated to the fight against Pediatric Blood Cancer...

Follow our journey at www.wrathbooks.com

CHAPTER 1

"TYLER, WHERE THE FUCK IS MY CHAI LATTE?" screamed Lefty Shapiro from his usual spot—hunched over the gigantic mahogany writing table in the corner of his magnificent office in Century Towers. With both fists planted firmly on the desktop, Lefty looked like an angry vulture preparing an attack on some poor unsuspecting prey. In such a pose, he was the epitome of one of Hollywood's most powerful super agents.

The Shapiro Agency, LTD was Lefty's pride and joy and he had built the business from the ground up. Perched high in the sky above downtown Los Angeles the Shapiro Agency took up the entire forty-fourth floor of Century Towers. The space resembled an airplane hangar more than a talent agency, with wide-open expanses exaggerated by the apparent lack of furnishings. That was the way Lefty liked things, the bigger the better. Everything he did was completely over the top. Even his realtor had questioned why he needed 20,000 square feet of office space for just him and his assistant *du jour*.

Lefty's corner office was no exception. Floor-to-ceiling windows surrounded the large room and on a clear day you could see all the way to the Hollywood Hills from one window and miles and miles of the Pacific Ocean from another. Of course, most of the time the panoramic views from Lefty's grand windows were hidden behind heavy clouds of dark thick smog. But what went on outside the walls of the Shapiro Agency was far less important than what went on inside them.

Marty Shapiro, or "Lefty" as the Hollywood elite knew him, was a power—player. He was a big, big cat and anyone that he represented was instantly shown the road to fame and fortune on their way to becoming a huge star. He made millions for his clients who included A-list celebrities, musicians and high-profile athletes; everyone in Hollywood wanted to work with him. He had his own table and standing reservations at LA's hottest restaurants and nightspots as well as memberships to all of the most prestigious clubs and golf courses. In his Rolodex were the private phone numbers and e-mail addresses of everyone who was anyone in Hollywood—*from Angelina to Zsa Zsa.*

But success had its price. Especially in the fast paced, hypocritical world of Hollywood stardom where things weren't always as they might appear. Indeed, Lefty could make you an overnight superstar, but he also had the power to take it all away. One call from Lefty and your career could be over in a flash. It was an awesome amount of power to have and Lefty made damn sure everyone who worked for him knew it. Such a reputation caused a great deal of discontent with Lefty in the industry. In fact, he was pretty much hated by just about everyone in the business, from the movie producers, to the studio execs, to the clients he represented. But, they all tolerated him because he made them money, a lot of money. Even the woman who cleaned Lefty's office found him intolerable. But there was no other way to the top in

Hollywood—step on a few toes, ruffle a few feathers or eliminate your competition. *It was kill or be killed.*

Lefty spent all of his days and most nights standing behind his desk or pacing his enormous office, barking orders into his wireless headset or in the direction of whichever personal assistant was attempting to suffer through the week. The shortest stint was that of a young, aspiring actress from the Midwest who had only lasted eight minutes; the record to beat was just over six days.

Tyler exhaled a long, drawn-out sigh. She took a deep breath and did her best to suppress the irritation in her voice. "Right away, Mr. Shapiro," she called out from the adjoining kitchenette.

The job of personal assistant to one of the 10 most powerful men in Hollywood sounded a lot better than it was actually turning out to be. Since responding to the advertisement in *Variety Magazine,* Tyler Paige had been brought to tears seven times by her boss's tirades, was sexually harassed on an hourly basis, had a clipboard thrown at her head by some obnoxious actress and had been scorched twice by steamed milk while trying to figure out Lefty's $20,000 cappuccino machine. It was only her third day.

Tyler shook her head and let out a sarcastic laugh. "Yeah, sure, right away you fat bastard," she mumbled under her breath as she carefully placed a ceramic mug under the spout of the gigantic machine, pressed the steam button and ducked for cover behind a chair. Suddenly, the machine sprung to life as the spout began making a loud hissing noise and then miraculously began scalding the milk into the mug without spraying it all over the room as it had traditionally done.

Tyler peered out from behind the chair and smiled. "Ha, I beat you. I finally beat you, you glorified coffee pot." She stood to her feet, did a little victory dance and then slowly made her way to the piping hot cup of tea. Cautiously, she peered into the mug and saw what appeared to be a perfect chai latte. Things were starting to look up. "Take that, Starbucks baristas," she said as she picked up the steaming mug and arranged it on a silver-serving tray along with the morning edition of *Variety*. She paused to check herself in the full-length mirror, which hung behind the kitchen door and frowned. "That won't do," she said disapprovingly as she gently set the tray down. She removed her hair clip and shook her head from side to side allowing her blond hair to fall carelessly over her shoulders. "Let's see if you can handle this, you fucking pervert," she said, as she hiked up her already short skirt and unbuttoned the top two buttons on her blouse, revealing her perfectly tanned cleavage and just a hint of lace from her black Victoria's Secret bra. Tyler smiled at her reflection. "There now, that's better," she said, as she reached for the tray and made her way down the hall to her boss's office.

Tyler Paige had grown up in east Los Angeles in what most would call a dysfunctional family. Her father died when she was a baby, and her mother never really got over his untimely death. For most of Tyler's life, her mother was addicted to one form of drug or another, and despite short stints in rehab, she never really got clean. She remarried a doctor, who eventually became her prescription pad drug dealer, but when his excessive drinking led to a black eye and sexual advances toward Tyler, he was quickly thrown to the curb.

Despite the adversity in her life, Tyler Paige managed to earn a scholarship to UCLA, where she graduated at the top of her class with a degree in business administration. She had done a bit of modeling during college, and with the money she earned made some wise investments in the stock market. Although she was 5'9" with naturally blond hair and a perfect body, she had no ambition to go the Hollywood starlet route. She wanted to be on the business end of Hollywood, producing movies, not acting in them; she wanted the money and she wanted the power. At 22, that's where Tyler Paige knew she was destined to wind up, even if it meant going down on that pig in the next room to get there.

Lefty's face was turning a deep shade of red and a vein was beginning to protrude along the side of his forehead as he frantically rifled through his Rolodex searching for a client's number. His eyes narrowed as he spotted the card and ripped it from the plastic fasteners. He let out a huff and then looked up from his desk in the direction of the door. "Tyler, if your skinny little ass is not in this office in three seconds, you can pack up your fucking desk and head back to that two-bit employment agency that sent you here!"

Tyler sighed. She took a deep breath and slowly opened the door with her free hand, making sure to keep the tray from crashing to the floor, like yesterday.

When she entered, Lefty was already on the phone screaming obscenities into the wireless headset that wrapped around his bald head. His face had turned magenta and the vein looked ready to burst at any moment. "Listen to me you little prick," he shouted, as he pointed his index finger at the imaginary person standing in front of him. "Stop snorting away the 25 million I got you for this picture and get your fucking ass to the set on time, or I'm gonna come down there and cut your goddamn balls off!" Lefty paused for effect. "Or else!" he shouted, and then hit the disconnect button on the headset without waiting for a reply.

In Hollywood, Lefty's "or else" meant you were about to be blacklisted from every major movie studio in town—perhaps the world. It meant no work—and to an actor, that was a fate worse than death. With one phone call, Lefty could make that happen. One day you're on top of the world drinking Cristal Champagne in a club with the Kardashian sisters, and the next you're back to waiting tables, dancing topless . . . or worse.

Lefty removed the headset and threw it in the direction of his desk. He looked at Tyler and frowned. "How fucking long does it take to make one goddamn cup of tea?" he said with a scowl, as he fell back into his leather desk chair.

Tyler desperately fought the urge to dump the latte over Lefty's bald head and managed to force an apologetic smile. "I'm so sorry, Mr. Shapiro," she said with a pout, as she suggestively leaned over his desk, placing the tray in front of him and making certain that he got a perfect view of her cleavage.

Lefty's eyes fixed on Tyler's breasts as he clumsily shuffled some papers back and forth on his desk. He cleared his throat. "Yes, well, be a little more considerate next time," he said, beads of sweat forming on his forehead.

Tyler grinned. "Oh, yes sir, I will," she said, as she slowly rose to an upright position. She tilted her head to the side allowing her hair to fall seductively across her face. "Will that be all, Mr. Shapiro?"

Lefty took a handkerchief from his trouser pocket and mopped up the sweat that had puddled on his brow. "Yes, yes, fine, fine," he said, as he began sorting through a bunch of papers.

Tyler smiled. "Very well, sir. I'll be at my desk if you need anything."

Lefty nodded without bothering to look up. "Fine, fine," he repeated, as he squeezed on a pair of bifocals and began reading through a memo FROM THE OFFICES OF STEVEN SPIELBERG: PERSONAL AND CONFIDENTIAL. Then he paused. He placed the memo back on his desk and peered over the top of his glasses at Tyler, who was approaching the door. "Ms. Paige, one more thing."

Tyler's smile widened but she made sure to conceal it as she turned to face her boss. *Fucking pervert.* "Yes, Mr. Shapiro?"

Lefty leaned back in his chair. He appeared more focused now. All business. "Set up a lunch meeting for this Friday at The Palms with Trevor Hash. You'll find his number in the Rolodex on your desk."

Tyler raised an eyebrow. "You mean thee Trevor Hash?" She hesitated. "Trevor Handsome Hash, the quarterback from USC?"

Lefty nodded. "Yeah, that Trevor Hash. Except he's about to become Trevor Handsome Hash, the new quarterback for the San Diego Chargers," replied Lefty with a confident grin.

Tyler's eyes narrowed. "Isn't he that cocky guy who talks about himself during interviews in the third person? Trevor Hash guarantees victory this Saturday!" she said, in a mimicking fashion. Then she giggled.

Lefty clasped his hands behind his head and leaned further back in his chair. "Yeah, he does. So what? A lot of these successful athletes do that." He paused and thought for a moment. "Chad Johnson from the Bengals, Terrell Owens from the Bills . . . ."

"Elmo from Sesame Street," interrupted Tyler.

Lefty frowned. He repositioned himself in front of his desk, and reached for the memo from Spielberg. "Oh, and another thing, Ms. Paige."

Tyler tilted her head to the side curiously. "Yes, Mr. Shapiro?"

Lefty adjusted his bifocals, flipped to the first page of the lengthy memo and began reading. "I'm gay."

Tyler's eyes widened. "Excuse me, sir."

Lefty flipped the page and continued reading. "You heard me right; I said I'm gay. You know, homosexual, a flamer. It's pretty common knowledge around town. Has been for years, actually."

Tyler's shoulders dropped. "I had no idea."

Lefty grinned. "Well, now you do." He looked up from the memo and gave Tyler a wink. "Hey, but great tits, baby."

Tyler frowned. "Thanks," she said in a defeated tone as she exited the room. She fell back onto the door as it closed behind her. She took a deep breath and as she exhaled, blew the hair from her face "This is going to be harder than I thought," she muttered, as she re-buttoned her blouse and made her way to her desk.

CHAPTER 2

IT WAS NEARLY 4 P.M. BY THE time Jake Chase finally returned to his downtown office at the Federal Bureau of Investigation's New York City headquarters. He'd been in and out of meetings all day, had lunch with the Sultan of Brunei and just finished a videoconference with the Secretary of Defense and the President of the United States—a pretty typical day. Ever since his promotion five months ago to Deputy Director of the FBI, Jake's life had become one long meeting after another. Most would consider being the youngest appointed Deputy Director in the history of the FBI the career opportunity of a lifetime, but Jake was finding it all too mundane. He missed the excitement of being in the field; he missed the action and most of all, Jake missed the daily adrenalin rush he got every day he went to work. But jumping out of an exploding helicopter and falling 30 feet into the East River probably wasn't the smartest thing to be doing, especially with his wife Diane pregnant with twins. It was time to slow down a bit. Time to play it safe.

Jake fell back into his desk chair, let out a long end-of-the-day sigh and gazed out at the Manhattan skyline. It was early fall, and the sky was already darkening as the sun descended across the Hudson River into New Jersey and the horizon. Jake frowned as he unclasped the top button on his collared shirt and loosened his tie—something else he couldn't get used to. He looked around his office and shook his head disapprovingly. The interior decorator had chosen a large, oak-wood desk with a matching credenza accompanied by a long row of towering bookshelves. She had lined two of the walls with black-and-white prints, all bearing some type of nautical theme, mostly ships and sailboats. The other two walls in the office were floor-to-ceiling glass and, in the corner, where the two rows of large windows met, she had constructed a formal sitting area. It was quite functional, with a large distressed leather couch situated across from two deep leather chairs separated by a small glass table. By the front door she had placed an oval-shaped conference table surrounded by black leather swivel chairs. In the center sat a steel replica of the *USS Constitution*. "Old World and very masculine," she had told him. When all was said and done, Jake had traded in dangerous missions in the Middle East for a corner power office on the 58th floor. He hated it.

Suddenly, Jake was awakened from his thoughts by a small red light flashing on his desk phone. He rubbed the tired from his eyes, then reached over and engaged the speaker phone. "Yes, Claudia," he said, as he loosened the knot on his tie even further.

"Mr. Chase, I have Michael Dumont here for you," came a woman's voice with a distinct British accent through the tiny speaker on the phone.

Jake smiled. Mike Dumont was one of his closest friends. He and Mike had both worked at the same law firm straight out of law school and had both suffered through the early years as young associates paying their dues together by clocking record-setting billable hours. Jake had left the firm more than 10 years ago to work for the bureau, but Mike had stayed on and had recently become a full partner. Although the two men were close, Jake hadn't seen or heard from his friend in more than 6 months. It was odd, but Jake figured it was most likely due to Mike's recent troubling divorce from his wife Anita.

There was a light tapping on the office door. Jake stood and made his way to the front of his desk. "Come in."

The door opened and Mike stepped in. He, too, was dressed in a suit and tie, but looked far more comfortable in his threads than Jake. In fact, at 6' 1" with dark curly hair and deep blue eyes, Michael Dumont looked like he could probably land a gig modeling his grey Armani pinstripe in the pages of *GQ*. Tall, dark and handsome, Mike's friends long ago had nicknamed him the "chick magnet"—most likely the reason for his recent divorce.

"Deputy Director Jake Chase. I do like the sound of that," Mike said, nodding his head approvingly as he gazed around the large room. "And the corner office on the 58th floor, not too shabby."

Michael Dumont was forever the status seeker. His winter car was a Mercedes Benz and his summer car a Ferrari. He had a different Rolex for every day of the week including weekends, and he only wore Armani suits, all of which were custom tailored privately for him at his home in exclusive Oyster Bay, Long Island. Thus, being appointed Deputy Director of the FBI was probably less important to Mike than the geographical positioning of the office that came with the job.

Jake's smile widened as he walked toward his friend. The two met, shook hands and then embraced. "How have you been?" asked Jake as he stepped back and gave Mike the once over. "I haven't seen you since the beginning of the summer."

Mike's smile vanished. "Has it really been that long?" Then he paused. "You know, this thing with Anita," he said, and his voice trailed off.

Jake gestured with his thumb in the direction of the couch. "Let's sit. We can catch up a bit." His voice was reassuring.

"Sure," Mike said, as he followed Jake to the corner of the room and fell back into one of the leather chairs.

Jake took a seat in the chair beside his friend.

"Man, it really is good to see you, Jake," Mike said. "We really can't let months go by like this without getting together."

Jake smiled, but couldn't help feeling bad for his old companion Mike, and to some extent, for Anita. The last 6 months had taken a toll on Mike and it showed. His eyes were shadowed and he looked tired, very tired. His handsome face appeared tight with stress. "Absolutely," Jake replied.

Mike leaned over and unzipped his briefcase. He reached in and pulled out a neatly wrapped rectangular shaped box. It was wrapped in silver foil and had a black ribbon tied around its top. Suddenly, he appeared melancholy as he placed the box on the glass table and slid it in Jake's direction.

Jake raised an eyebrow. "What's this?" he asked, shaking his head as he lifted the box from the table. He opened a small card that was taped to the front and read the inscription. *To my dear friend Jake, "A man cannot be comfortable without his own approval." Michael.* It was a quote from Mark Twain; is this how Mike has been feeling over the past several months? Jake wondered as he stared at the small card. He then looked up at his friend. "This really wasn't necessary."

Mike placed his elbows on his knees and leaned forward. "Yes, it absolutely was," he replied, his voice deliberate now. Then he hesitated for a moment, took a deep breath and continued. "I've been beating myself up for months, Jake. My best friend is appointed Deputy Director of the FBI and I don't even show up to congratulate him." Another hesitation, followed by another deep breath. "I'd say this is more than overdue."

"Yeah," replied Jake. "But I know you were going through some very . . . ."

"No! No, doesn't matter," interrupted Mike. "Should never let a woman come between friends. Even if that woman is your wife. Um, I mean ex-wife," he said, and his voice faded into the room.

Jake looked back down at the card and re-read Twain's words. He couldn't imagine what his friend was going through. At one time, the four had been such good friends. Diane and Anita had become close when Jake and Mike were young associates at the firm, and a real bond developed between them. In the beginning, the four would often go to dinner or to the movies or out for cocktails. They would spend weekends together at Diane's beach house in the Hamptons, often speaking of how their children, when they had them, would have so much fun together at the beach. And even when Jake left the practice, they all managed to stay close. That was, of course, until 6 months ago when everything seemed to unravel in both men's lives. Jake's last assignment nearly got him and Diane killed and had landed Diane in the hospital with a broken leg. Her father, multi-millionaire Jack Sheppard, had been brutally murdered only 3 years before in his Malibu beach house. When the killer came back for Diane, things ended in a bloody shootout in the family home. The horrible twist was that Jake's boss, friend and mentor, former FBI Deputy Director Ken Devasher, had somehow been associated with the killer. When all was said and done, Devasher had vanished with nearly 100 million dollars. Despite a 6 month worldwide manhunt, there wasn't a single lead on the whereabouts Devasher or the money.

Jake let out a long sigh and slowly looked up from the card. "You know, Diane and I called you almost every day."

Mike nodded. "I know you did, Jake."

Jake's eyes narrowed. "The last time I saw you and Anita was in the hospital when Diane's leg was broken. You both seemed happy."

Mike shook his head and relaxed back into his chair. "Beats the heck out of me. One day we're walking on the beach and she turns to me and says she needs some time apart. Says we really don't communicate anymore. Blames the law firm and all the time I spend at the office."

Jake frowned and let out a sarcastic laugh. "Yeah, I know that conversation pretty well."

"Last I heard she's back in Chicago living with her sister." Mike paused and gazed out the window. The sun was almost completely down and the lights on the buildings began to glow in the crisp night sky. He took a deep breath and looked back at Jake with a crooked smile. "The funny thing about it is that she could have really taken me to the cleaners financially. You know what she wanted in the divorce?"

Jake stayed silent.

Mike shook his head in disbelief. "Our wedding album. That's it. Can you fucking believe it? Our goddamn wedding album." He fell quiet and looked out the window again still shaking his head. "She could have had millions," he said, his voice much lower now, "but all she took was our fucking wedding album. "Said it reminded her of the happiest time in her life."

Jake reached over and placed his hand on his friend's shoulder. Mike's eyes narrowed and suddenly a smile stretched across his face. He took a deep breath and exhaled slowly. "It's time to move on," he said.

"Yes, I believe it is, my friend," Jake replied, as he reached for the box Mike had given him and began to unwrap the foil. "I assume this isn't the complete works of Mark Twain."

Mike relaxed deep into his chair, clasped his hands behind his head and smiled. "No, something a bit more practical than that."

Jake opened the box and peered inside. It was a bottle of Louie Tre. The least expensive bottle, which this wasn't, went for about $3,000. Jake shook his head as he removed it from the box. "Indeed it is," he said, staring at the bottle. "Indeed it is."

The two men stood to their feet and shook hands. "Thank you, Mike. It really is a generous gift," said Jake.

Mike smiled and pulled Jake in for a hug. "No, Jake, thank you," he said, and then his smile widened. It was as if he had gone through some kind of miraculous transformation. Somehow, during the conversation the old Mike had suddenly resurfaced. The darkness under his eyes had vanished, and his usual air of confidence had returned. "I say we crack that sucker and see what all the fuss is about."

"Absolutely," Jake replied, as he reached for the phone and dialed the extension for Claudia. He summoned her to bring two drinking glasses and a small bucket of ice.

"Right away, Mr. Chase."

Mike wandered over to the corner windows and looked down at the city below which seemed to be bustling with an abundance of nocturnal activity. Rows of cars illuminated the long gridiron of streets and avenues that intertwined with one another throughout the island of Manhattan. In the distance Mike could see a well-lit construction site with trucks and cranes seemingly moving in slow motion in every direction. It all appeared quite peaceful from high in the sky.

"You can really see everything from up here," Mike said, as Jake joined him by the window.

Jake nodded. Then he pointed to the construction site. "There's where the World Trade Center used to be." He paused. "They finally began construction on the Freedom Tower."

Mike gave Jake an awkward smile.

Jake's dad had been a firefighter. One of New York's bravest, he was killed in the September 11th tragedy but not before saving 7 people. He had been crushed to death rushing into Tower Two to save an 8th, shortly before it collapsed. He was a hero.

Jake stepped back from the window and looked at his friend. "Like you said, Mike, it's time to move on."

Suddenly, there was a knock. "Time for that drink," Jake said, as he walked in the direction of the door. Then he stopped momentarily, looked back at Mike, and frowned. "And for God's sake, loosen that fucking tie, will ya?" he said with a laugh.

As Jake approached the door it slowly swung open and in walked Diane, carrying a small ice bucket and two glasses. She was dressed casually in a pair of faded jeans and a hand-knit, crew neck sweater that protruded over her belly. Her hair was pulled back in a tight pony tail and she was smiling. She had a smile that lit up her whole face.

Dr. Diane Chase was a tall woman and in her earlier years had done some modeling for Calvin Klein. She was in her mid-30s and was a striking woman both in personality and in looks.

From the moment Mike had resurfaced, Diane insisted on coming in for today's little meeting. Jake had agreed, but decided not to mention it to Mike. He knew Mike would want to see Diane but wasn't sure if her presence would accentuate the missing Anita.

Jake greeted her with a hug and a kiss on her lips. "Hey, Di Di," he said, as she rubbed her nose against his like an Eskimo, something she had been doing since the two started dating in high school.

She pulled back and gave Jake a questioning look. "How's he doing?" she whispered.

Jake gave a nod as they both turned to face Mike, who appeared to be very happy to see her. Jake quietly breathed a sigh of relief as Diane handed him the glasses and the ice bucket and then walked slowly in Mike's direction.

"Michael Dumont," she said affectionately and embraced him in a warm hug. "We've missed you terribly."

Mike gave Jake a knowing look over Diane's shoulder. *Ambushed!* Jake grinned as he placed the ice bucket and the glasses down on his desk. "So, how 'bout those drinks?"

Diane stepped back from Mike and gave him a warm smile. Suddenly, Mike's eyes widened as he slapped the palm of his hand against his forehead. He looked shocked as he stood motionless staring at Diane's mid-section. Then he uttered a single word. It was no louder than a whisper. "Pregnant."

Diane's smile widened and she looked over at Jake.

Mike brought his other hand to his forehead as he slowly looked up. "I can't believe I forgot," he said, in sad and apologetic tones, looking back and forth between Jake and Diane. He was visibly upset.

Diane had discovered she was pregnant shortly before Mike and Anita had split up. The four had celebrated the news together over a wonderful dinner at a private club Mike belonged to in New York City. Uncle Mike and Auntie Anita were going to be the godparents. "The first of many," Mike had said in a spontaneous toast, and had then leaned into Jake and whispered, "and may they all be boys." That was six months ago.

Jake cleared his throat. "Look, Mike," he said, as he grabbed the glasses and walked towards his friend. "For lack of a better phrase, shit happens." Then he paused and looked at Diane. "To everyone." He took a deep breath and exhaled slowly. "But what's important is that when it does, we're able to pick ourselves up by the bootstraps and get back in the game. And that's what you did."

"Yes," said Diane, placing her hand on her tummy. "And just in the nick of time. I mean, it's like the ninth inning."

Jake handed Mike one of the glasses and placed a hand on his shoulder. He gripped tightly and gave Mike a shake back and forth. "Yeah, just in time to change diapers, Uncle Mike."

Mike laughed. "It's really great to have friends like you both."

Jake smiled and released Mike's shoulder. He picked up the bottle of cognac, looked at the label and shook his head. He uncorked the top and poured out two generous portions.

Diane raised an eyebrow. "Want to hear the best part?"

Mike's eyes narrowed. "Best part?"

Diane looked at Jake and smiled. "We're having twins."

Mike's jaw dropped. "That's incredible."

Jake let out a small chuckle as he swirled the caramel-colored liquid around inside his glass. He leaned in and inhaled the woody aroma. *Not bad for 40 bucks a sip.* "Wanna hear the real best part?" he added.

Mike stayed silent. He was still smiling.

Jake looked up from his glass. A grin stretched across his face. "Twin boys."

Suddenly, Mike's face lit up even more. "Twin boys! Did you just say twin boys!" He let out celebratory cheer. "*Waa-Hoo!* I cannot believe it, twin friggin' b . . ." Suddenly he stopped shouting and his face became serious. He took a deep breath, regained his composure and looked at Diane. "I mean, not that there would be anything wrong with girls."

Diane laughed.

The smile re-appeared on Mike's face. "Well, you're right about one thing, Diane. I did get back just in the nick of time." He looked over and gave Jake a wink. "I mean, someone's gotta teach these guys how to catch a football," he joked as he leaned in and gave her a big hug and a kiss on the cheek. Next it was Jake's turn. This time, a huge bear hug as he murmured the words, "Twin friggin' boys!" in Jake's ear.

Mike stepped back and raised his glass of cognac. Jake raised his, and Diane, a bottle of water she had retrieved from her backpack. "To my best friends and their twin sons. May they both grow up to be healthy, strong leaders, just like their old man."

"Yes," said Diane. "And to Jake's new job as the youngest-ever appointed Deputy Director of the FBI." She turned and faced him. "I'm so proud of you." Then she paused. "And, most importantly, to no more field-work and no more dangerous missions!"

"Here, here," said Mike.

The room fell quiet as all eyes fell upon Jake.

"Yes," Jake repeated, trying his best to sound enthusiastic. "No more missions."

Mike looked at his friend inquisitively as Diane gave Jake a sad smile.

Jake took a deep breath and raised his glass higher. A grin returned to his face, heightening his boyish good looks. "To friendship," he said, as he drank up 70 dollars worth.

"To friendship," repeated Mike and Diane in unison.

CHAPTER 3

IT WAS ALMOST 7 P.M. BY THE TIME Jake and Diane had arrived back at their Bedford home in Westchester County. The house originally belonged to Diane's father, Jack Sheppard. Diane, his only child, inherited the house after his untimely death three years ago. Old Captain Jack had bought the home in the early 80's from fashion magnate Gloria Vanderbilt and used it mostly as a retreat to entertain high-end clients, politicians and celebrities. The original structure was a mere 12,000 square feet, but Jack immediately added an extension bigger than most people's homes, along with a pool house, a guest cottage, and a separate five-car garage to keep his Ferrari collection.

In addition to the house, Jake and Diane had inherited several hundred million dollars, an entire floor in Trump Towers in New York City, an East Coast beach house in Southampton, a West Coast beach house in Malibu and a Gulfstream G5 to dart between them in record time.

After some convincing, Mike had agreed to follow Jake and Diane up to the house for dinner. He had originally proposed treating at the Water Club, but Diane had insisted that Mike looked like he could use a good home-cooked meal—a point he couldn't argue. The drive from the city was only about 50 minutes, but Jake drove an Aston Martin DB9 and Mike a brand new 7-series Beamer—so a half-hour later, the three were walking up the grand stairs leading to the front entrance.

Mike made his way through the front door and shook his head in awe. "This place looks bigger every time I'm here." He smiled and gave Jake a nod. "So what's it like living in a 20,000 square foot castle?"

Diane frowned. "It's not quite that big," she said. She paused and looked at Jake. Her eyes spoke volumes of the sadness she still felt for the loss of her father. She looked at Mike and forced a smile. "Well, you know my dad. He took everything to extremes."

As awareness of Diane's grief descended on Mike, he froze in place and stared at the ground with his coat dangling off one arm. *Open mouth, insert foot.* Slowly, he raised his head and gave Diane an awkward smile. "Well, you know 20,000 square feet may not be enough room once those twin boys are born."

Diane smiled. She took Mike's overcoat and placed it on a hanger in the foyer closet. "Very funny" she said, as she proceeded through the two-story entranceway in the direction of the kitchen.

Captain Jack's house was a Tudor-style home set far back off a private road on 15 acres in one of the most exclusive neighborhoods in the world. Anyone who lived in one of the estates along Schoolhouse Road in Bedford had to have done something pretty special to get there. On one side, the neighbors were the Carlins, a billionaire hedge-fund family, and on the other, Calvin Klein. Each of the six families that resided along Schoolhouse made the Forbes 400 richest Americans list year after year, and since Jack's death, Diane and Jake ranked number 27.

Jake shook his head as he hung his coat next to Mike's in the closet. "Yeah, hysterical, man," he said. Then he shot Mike a grin. "Remember, you're gonna learn to change diapers, pal."

Mike laughed as the two men followed Diane into the kitchen. It was a large room, well lit by two symmetrical rows of bay windows, with a magnificent set of French doors that led out to a stone patio. The room was divided in half by a long limestone snack bar. On one side was an area for food preparation with multiple cooktops, ovens, and sinks. The industrial look resembled that of a kitchen set-up in a restaurant or glamorous hotel. On the other side of the snack bar a round wooden table was centered in front of the French doors. The tabletop was inlaid with what appeared to be a million tiny ceramic tiles, all forming a decorative mosaic. It looked very expensive.

Jake hung his suit jacket neatly over one of the chairs at the table. He looked at Mike and gestured to one of the bar stools. "Grab a seat. I'll get us a few beers," he said, as he exited the room in the direction of Jack's office.

Mike gave an abbreviated salute and hopped onto one of the stools at the snack bar. Diane leaned over the island and faced Mike, stretching her arms over the limestone surface. She tapped her finger against her lip, considering. Then she looked at Mike. "Pasta?"

"Sounds great."

Still resting on her forearms, she called after Jake. "How do you feel about pasta and homemade sauce?"

"Sounds great," he shouted back.

The room that once served as Jack's office was well appointed and masculine in design. Along one wall was a row of built-in bookshelves filled with classics. *Moby Dick, The Scarlet Letter, Of Mice and Men* were among the many prominently displayed novels in Jack's collection. Some of the books were leather bound and others were first editions, all contributing to the impressive setting for which Jack had aimed. Across the room, set against the far wall was a mahogany credenza in front of which sat a leather-topped writing table, both prominently displaying a host of trophies, awards and autographed pictures Jack had acquired during his years producing movies in Hollywood.

Jake walked to the credenza and knelt down in front of an autographed photo of Jack with his arm around an aging Frank Sinatra. Both men were wearing tuxedoes and appeared to be at some sort of an awards ceremony. Jake glanced at the photo, shook his head and chuckled. He then pressed the two doors at the front of the credenza. There was a clicking sound as the inner locks released and the doors gently sprung open. Inside, was a small stack of compact discs, set beside a state-of-the-art Bose music system. Jake reached in and grabbed the disc at the top of the stack—*Billy Joel's Greatest Hits, Volume I.* He opened the case and popped the CD into the player. Suddenly, the crisp sound of a harmonica, belting out the melody to *Piano Man*, was playing through speakers in every room in the house.

Jake smiled as the distinct sound of Billy Joel's voice echoed throughout the study. *Sing us a song you're the piano man . . .* "Perfect."

He stood and walked to a formal sitting area at the far corner of the room. A dark leather couch and two matching chairs sat neatly across from one another, centered on a blood-red Persian carpet. It created a pleasing barrier between a large bay window that looked out over the pool and the rows of bookshelves. In front of the window was a wet bar with a built-in mini refrigerator. Jake grabbed two Heinekens from the fridge and made his way back to the kitchen.

As Jake entered the room, he noticed that Mike and Diane had already begun dinner preparations. Mike was still sitting at the snack bar but now had lost the tie and his sleeves were rolled up to his elbows. He was busy dicing plump red tomatoes on a large wooden cutting board.

Diane was standing in front of the main stove. She had her back to the rest of the kitchen as she added a chopped sweet onion to a large copper pot that was sitting above a low flame. She looked over her shoulder at Jake and smiled. "Good choice," she said, nodding in the direction of one of the small speakers mounted in the kitchen ceiling.

"Thanks," replied Jake, as he placed one of the green bottles down on the snack bar beside the cutting board. "Here ya go, Emeril," he joked and then settled into one of the chairs at the table.

Mike gave Jake a wink, slowly lifted the cutting board and carefully made his way to the stove. "Ready for these?" he asked

Diane nodded.

Mike rested the cutting board on the side of the pot and angled it downward, allowing the pile of diced tomatoes to fall into the sauce. He grabbed a towel that was folded neatly over the handle of one of the ovens and wiped his hands dry. "The Rangers start their season tonight," he said, as he picked up his beer and sat down at the kitchen table across from Jake. "The firm has a skybox at the Garden," he continued, and then took a big swig from his beer. "We should catch a few games this season."

Jake smiled. "Sure, man. You know how much I love hockey. Especially Rangers hockey."

As a boy, Jake and his brother Mattie grew up playing ice hockey on a small pond in their backyard in Jersey City. Winter and fall at the Chase residence were for hockey and football, while spring and summer were reserved for baseball and lacrosse. Both Chase boys were very athletic and both continued to play sports through college. Matt at West Point and Jake at NYU. Although Jake would never pass up hockey at The Garden, he still preferred to be in the stands with the real fans, rather than in some silly luxury skybox. But the deputy director of the FBI couldn't be seen in the cheap seats, especially with the celebrity status Jake had begrudgingly acquired over the last five months.

Solving the Paramount case had indeed put Jake on the map, but killing Nuri Irgashev, the mastermind behind one of the worst assaults since the World Trade Center disaster bombing, right there in old Jack's study, made Jake Chase a household name. Just add Jake's predecessor, mentor, and one time good friend, former Deputy Director Ken Devasher, vanishing with 100 million dollars of Irgashev's money, and you had the perfect movie script.

Over the past six months, Jake had received numerous offers from a multitude of Hollywood agents, movie producers, and studio execs. He had been invited to appear on every talk show from *The View* to *The Tonight Show*, but had graciously declined them all. However, he did regret turning down Letterman.

Jake took a swig from the bottle as he relaxed into his chair. Diane covered the pot, which was now simmering on the stove, and joined the two men at the kitchen table. Her hair was tied into a loose knot and she was wearing a dishtowel over her left shoulder. She frowned and nodded in the direction of Jake's beer. "Boy, what I would give for one of those," she said.

Jake smiled at her and slid his beer across the table. "I don't think one sip is gonna hurt anybody."

Diane grinned. "Where's the fun in one sip?" she said, with a wink in Mike's direction. She then reached over to her bag which was hanging on the back of one of the barstools and pulled out a bottle of water. She looked down at the square shaped container and sighed. "Three months," she muttered to herself and then took a big sip. She looked up at Mike and Jake. "Yeah, yeah, all right," she said laughingly. "Enjoy your beers. I'm going to take a shower. We'll eat in about an hour," she continued, as she stood up bracing her back with the palms of her hands. "Why don't you guys go shoot some hoops?"

Mike's head perked up. "Did you say hoops?"

Diane chuckled. "Yeah, hoops. We did a little updating to Daddy's tennis court," she said, slowly making her way around the table to the French doors. "Have a look," she said as she turned on a long row of light switches.

Suddenly, the entire backyard sprang to life as hundreds of small lanterns lit up the gardens, pergolas, guest cottage and pool house with a warm and subtle glow. The look was in one word, awesome. And why wouldn't it be? After all, old Jack had paid a small fortune for an army of landscape architects, engineers, stone masons and gardeners to create the perfect setting for entertaining clients, business associates, Hollywood celebrities and politicians; all the usual suspects.

Situated beside one of the cottages was a swimming pool, the likes of which rivaled even the most exclusive of resorts. At the far corner, a raised spa spilled pool water over a stone waterfall that caused shimmering ripples to, somewhat hypnotically, disturb the dark water below. The pool's black painted bottom was illuminated by underwater fluorescent lights that cast a dark hue and were dancing shadows on the white pines that line the property.

Just beyond the swimming pool, six stadium-type lampposts rose high into the night sky and shone down onto a full length basketball court.

Mike's jaw dropped. "It's like fucking Disney World for adults!"

Diane laughed. "Yeah, a company called Sports Courts came in, and in two days converted Daddy's tennis court into an all-sports court."

Mike stood and walked to the French doors. "All sports?"

Diane nodded and joined him by the doors. "Yup," she said, "tennis, volleyball, full-court basketball and enough room for a good rollerblade workout."

Mike shook his head. "I'm sold. Where do I get one?"

Diane gave Jake a smile. "I'll throw down some sweats and a few pairs of sneakers," she said, as she slowly made her way to the back staircase at the far end of the kitchen.

Jake polished off the rest of his beer, stood and gave a big stretch. "Come on, I'll spot you 10 points," he said to Mike. He unlocked the door and the two proceeded onto the stone patio and walked in the direction of the pool.

Mike shook his head in amazement. "This place really is like a fucking resort," he said.

Jake tucked both hands in his two front pockets. *Probably waited a bit too long to have the pool closed,* he thought to himself. With the sun down, the brisk night air was a reminder that as unusually warm as the season had been, it was early fall. "Yeah, old Jack didn't mess around."

Mike winced. "Speaking of Diane's father, how have things been since, ya know, the incident?"

By "the incident" Mike was referring to The Paramount Studios case, Jake's final assignment as an FBI field agent. In a bizarre turn of events, the terrorists responsible for killing hundreds in the bombing of Paramount Studios in Los Angeles had been none other than the same men who murdered Jack in his home in Malibu two years earlier. Both the bombing and the murder turned out to be acts of revenge. The odd twist was that Nuri Irgashev, the group's leader and the man solely responsible for killing Jack, broke into the Bedford house and held Diane at gunpoint. Luckily, Diane was able to free her hand and grab a letter opener from Jack's writing table, which she drove into her captor, giving Jake an opportunity to put four bullets into his head.

Jake sighed as the two men made their way through a gate onto the court. "We really don't discuss it much, but I think Diane finally has some closure and has made peace with her father's death."

Mike stayed silent.

Jake pointed toward the sidelines, about mid-court, to a tall wooden chair.

Mike looked at the chair, then looked back at Jake. "Referee's seat?"

Jake nodded. "Yeah, it was a gift to Diane's father. Read the inscription," he said, nodding at a small plaque affixed to one of the chair legs.

Jack, you beat me seven straight sets. You bastard! It was signed, *Henry Kissinger.*

Mike's eyes widened. "Henry Kissinger gave this to Jack?"

"Yup, this backyard certainly has seen . . . ."

Suddenly, Jake's BlackBerry went off. It vibrated twice and then stopped, indicating an e-mail rather than a phone call. He reached down and removed the device from his belt, looked at the display screen, but didn't recognize the sender. Somehow someone had breached FBI security and had gotten hold of Jake's private e-mail account. Slowly he scrolled through the text, but could not believe what he was reading.

Violets are blue,
Roses are red.
In exactly one hour
A Hollywood starlet
Will lose her head!

CAN YOU STOP ME, AGENT CHASE?
The message was signed, The Artist.

Jake glanced at his watch, 7:20. He took a deep breath and briefly closed his eyes. He rubbed his forehead. Someone was sending him a warning—or was it a challenge? But why? Why him? He opened his eyes and looked down at the screen one last time before placing the Blackberry back into its leather holster. His face was far more serious with the relaxed atmosphere of a quiet dinner long, long gone. He clenched his teeth and briefly glanced in the direction of his friend. "I'm really sorry Mike, but something has just come up and I need to get to LA immediately," Jake said, quickly exiting the All-Sports Court and dashing toward the house.

Mike's shoulders dropped. "Is everything okay, Jake?"

"No. No it's not!"

CHAPTER 4

SITTING IN THE BACK OF THE University of Southern California's media room, The Artist watched in utter disgust as throngs of reporters packed themselves into the overcrowded room, all for the chance to suck up to the mighty superstar, Trevor Hash. How pathetic it all seemed. It actually made him feel sick to his stomach—completely nauseous. He wanted to puke right there all over the floor in front of him.

Clenching his fists tightly, he sensed he was fast approaching that dangerous point once again, the point of no return. He could feel himself beginning to lose control as his head started to pound and the vein by his temple began to throb uncontrollably. He closed his eyes and tried to control his breathing, but it was no use. He could hear his heart pounding with a beat that echoed throughout his brain. His jaw hurt from clenching his teeth, and he was beginning to hear the voices again. *This was bad, very bad.*

He reached inside his blazer pocket and pulled out a small bottle of pills. He quickly twisted off the cap, tilted his head back and poured in a mouthful. As he chewed the medicine, he closed his eyes and slowly began rubbing his temples. "In due time, superstar," he said under his breath, desperately fighting the urge to charge into the locker room and beat him to death with his football helmet. "Stick with the plan," he told himself. "Control the urges, stick with the plan and you'll be the superstar."

He took a deep breath, and when he opened his eyes the entire room seemed to be moving in slow motion. The pills were working. Thank God she had given him the pills. The irritating voices surrounding him now all seemed to blend together in a mellow hum, as if everyone was talking under water.

"Ah, that's so much better," he said as the pounding in his head began to subside and his breathing became more regular. "So much better." He looked down at his watch, nearly 4:30 PM.

Reaching under his seat, The Artist picked up a black leather case and brought it to his lap. He unzipped one of the side compartments and took out a BlackBerry PDA he had recently borrowed from a student's book bag. He powered it on and toggled to the e-mail window. There was only one address he had entered: FBI Deputy Director, Jake Chase. Getting Deputy Director Chase's private e-mail address was no easy task, but with the right connections and enough money, you could accomplish just about anything.

The Artist stared down at the screen for a long moment. He seemed almost mesmerized by the name: Jake Chase. He could feel his hand tighten around the PDA as he again clenched his teeth. He reached inside his pocket, grabbed the bottle of pills and quickly downed another mouthful. He took a deep breath and looked back down at the name on the screen: Jake Chase. "Ha," he cackled, shaking his head in disgust. "Youngest Deputy Director ever appointed. *Time Magazine's* Man of the Year. What a fucking joke that was!" he scowled. "Well, deputy director, Paramount may have made you famous, but what I have in store will make you infamous," he muttered, as he began to type.

> VIOLETS ARE BLUE,
> ROSES ARE RED.
> IN EXACTLY ONE HOUR
> A HOLLYWOOD STARLET
> WILL LOSE HER HEAD!
> CAN YOU STOP ME, AGENT CHASE?

The Artist then hit the send button, smiled, and relaxed into his chair. He saw that Trevor Hash was now being introduced by the school's athletic director and was being ushered onto the stage. Coach Joe Rinaldi accompanied him along with two burly men The Artist did not recognize. He reached back into his case and retrieved his personal PDA and scrolled through the icons, double-clicking on the one marked "notes." He read through the many entries, mostly names of celebrities, politicians and athletes, with the exception of the Deputy Director. He settled the cursor on the entry titled "Handsome" and clicked. Suddenly, pages and pages of notes on Trevor Hash appeared on the screen—meticulously detailed notes that covered everything from favorite restaurants to blood type. He scrolled to the last page of the dossier and began to type. *Thursday, October 2, 2009—two bodyguards—both over 6 feet tall—expensive suits—no doubt hired by Lefty Shapiro. Pretty standard.*

Just then Trevor approached the podium causing the entire room to fall silent. The only noise was the sound of The Artist's chair screeching along the floor as he stood and quickly exited the room. He had seen enough, and once again he had flown under their radar, hadn't he?

Although he stood over 6' tall and had shoulder length, jet-black hair which he wore pulled tightly off his face in a neat ponytail, The Artist fit right in. That was the one thing he had become quite proficient at—fitting in. Whether it was the annual convention of street sweepers or the Presidential Inaugural Ball, The Artist had a way of blending in with the masses, and today's press conference at USC was no exception.

With a little help from the internet and a color laser printer, he had created his own press pass to clip to his lapel. Add a pair of khakis, a dark turtleneck, and a herringbone tweed blazer, the kind with the patches on the elbows, and voila, instant reporter.

The Artist approached the exit to the media room but stopped momentarily for one last look. He let out a sarcastic chuckle. "Priceless," he said. He then angled his PDA in the direction of the podium, zoomed in on Trevor's face and quickly snapped off a picture. He looked down at the display screen that now revealed a close-up photo of Trevor Hash's cocky grin. "Perfect," he mumbled to himself, as he saved the photo in a PDF file he had named Pride. There were at least 30 other pictures stored in Pride, mostly A-list celebrities, athletes and, of course, Jake Chase.

All part of the plan, he thought, as he made his way into the visitor parking lot behind the USC locker room. Still holding his PDA with one hand, he reached into his pant pocket with the other and retrieved the key to his car, a 1998 Ford Taurus. He pointed the key in the direction of the windshield and pressed a small button on the key ring. The car emitted a loud chirping sound indicating that the alarm had been disengaged, not that anyone in Hollywood would bother to steal a 1998 Ford Taurus. The Artist climbed into the driver's seat, threw his leather bag in the back and returned to the Pride file. Slowly, he began to toggle through his photo gallery of Hollywood movers and shakers. Each and every one would propel him to stardom. Of course, to accomplish this, each and every one would be a victim of the most gruesome killing spree to hit Los Angeles since the Charles Manson murders. But what are you gonna do—this is Hollywood.

The first photo in the gallery was of Super Agent Lefty Shapiro, hunched over a lectern at last year's Academy Awards. He was wearing a tuxedo that looked like it was two sizes too small, and he appeared to be sweating through the collar. The Artist laughed cruelly at the picture. "You fat bastard," he said mockingly. "I should change the name of this file to Gluttony." He toggled to the next photo. It was a voyeuristic shot of Hollywood's hottest new starlet, Brooklyn Sims, topless, sunning herself by her swimming pool at her Hollywood Hills mansion. The Artist couldn't help but notice how her long auburn hair, clipped back in a silky swirl of golden red, accented her beautiful face. She was breathtaking. "What a shame it will be to remove that pretty little head of yours, Brooke baby," he said, as he toggled to the next photo in the queue. Suddenly, a smile came to his face. "Ah, but I will take great pleasure in removing yours," he said, laughing out loud as he gazed upon the photo of bad boy Jesse James, lead singer of LA's hottest new band, The Ravens. The smile quickly faded as the next photo appeared on the screen. The Artist felt his heart begin to race and his hands start to tremble as he looked down at the picture. Through clenched teeth he whispered the name, "Jake Chase."

CHAPTER 5

TREVOR "HANDSOME" HASH HAD THE WORLD BY THE BALLS. At 6'4", 240 pounds of lean muscle, he was the quintessential college football quarterback, and not just any college either. Trevor Hash was the star QB for the University of Southern California Trojans, and last year he led his team to an undefeated season and a national championship, earning himself the Heisman Trophy. He was strikingly handsome, and *Sports Illustrated*, in last month's cover article, referred to him as a young Muhammad Ali look-alike. Not bad for a sophomore.

"Trevor, any predictions on Saturday's game with the Fighting Irish?" a female correspondent shouted from the back of the overcrowded pressroom at USC stadium.

Gazing out over the throngs of reporters, Trevor could barely make out where the question had come from, let alone which one of the hundreds of reporters had asked it. From where he stood, positioned on stage behind the USC podium, Trevor squinted out over the crowd in the direction he believed the voice had originated. Standing on stage along with Trevor was USC Head Coach Joe Rinaldi, Athletic Director Chuck Gilberti, and two men who looked completely out of place, dressed in very expensive Giorgio Armani suits—the Rossi brothers. Both men were employed by the Shapiro Agency and had been Trevor's shadow ever since he signed with Lefty three days ago. They looked more like Mafioso than employees of the hottest talent agency in Los Angeles.

It was a Thursday afternoon in the fall, which meant only one thing—football season was under way at USC, and as usual the press room was bursting at the seams with media from all parts of the country. Every reporter in the room was dying to get the exclusive with Trevor Hash. Of course, every one of them had the same two questions: Would USC stage a repeat of last year's season and win the National Championship? And more importantly, would Trevor be returning next year, or would he be signing with a pro team? However, Trevor had to swear under the penalty of death, probably at the hands of the Rossi brothers, not to disclose the answer to the second of those two questions until Lefty gave him the green light.

"Media Thursdays," as it had been appropriately named by the USC Athletic Department, was the day that everyone from ESPN's Sports Center, down to and including even the smallest news stations, descended upon USC for the scoop on the upcoming game from Southern Cal's coaches and players or "player", as the case might be.

It had been that way for as long as Trevor could remember. Even during Pop Warner football, the local media in Buxom, Missouri, where Trevor was born and raised by his grandmother, Nanny Mary, all fought for the opportunity to speak to him about what many called a gift unparalleled by any other athlete. Of course, to get to Trevor, you had to first go through Nanny Mary, which was just about as difficult as getting through the Rossi brothers.

Nanny Mary would have none of that nonsense. *"Your studies and church come first—no exceptions!"* she would say affectionately but sternly. *"Then, if there's time, you can play that dangerous game with your friends."*

Trevor's parents were killed in a drive-by shooting when Trevor was a young boy. It was a senseless shootout between two rival high schools that took both his parents' lives, just because they happened to be in the wrong place at the wrong time. At five years old, Trevor found himself all alone in the world. The moment Nanny Mary got the news, she packed her bags and moved to Buxom to care for Trevor, and it had been that way ever since.

Trevor held his hand in front of his face and squinted his eyes against the glare of the camera lights. "I'm sorry, who asked that question?" He said in the general direction the voice had come from.

"Hi, Trevor, Naomi Brown, *Sports News Today*," replied a pretty young reporter, raising her hand and smiling in his direction.

"There you are. My, my, you certainly are a hot little thing, aren't you, Naomi Brown?" he said in his usual arrogant manner, as the field of reporters began chuckling amongst themselves at his remark. "You must be new. Didn't anyone bother to tell you the rules? Didn't you get the memo?"

"Here we go," whispered one of the reporters who was sitting in the front row, to his camera man. Then he chuckled. "Get ready for another priceless Trevor Hash interview."

The female reporter looked dumfounded. She appeared mortified as the chuckles from the crowd grew even louder. "I don't understand," she mumbled under her breath. Just then, another female reporter who was standing behind her, leaned forward and whispered in Naomi's ear. "He doesn't answer female reporters unless you call him by his nickname."

Naomi deflated. She let out a sigh and then looked back up at the podium. "Handsome," she paused. Another sigh. "Any predictions on Saturday's game against the Irish?"

Trevor grinned. "Well, Naomi Brown, Trevor's glad you asked him that question. It's like this, baby girl. Trevor Hash hasn't lost a football game in the past three years, and Trevor Hash don't plan on losing one this year either."

The room began to buzz with excitement. Trevor's words were beginning to stir the room into a frenzy. The only two people who didn't appear excited, besides the Rossi brothers, were the USC head coach and the athletic director. They both appeared a bit concerned with Trevor's promise.

Just then a voice broke through the chattering reporters. "You mean you don't plan on losing this weekend, dontcha, Handsome? I mean you can't be making a prediction on the rest of the season."

Suddenly Trevor's smile vanished and his face became deathly serious. "Who asked that?" he demanded as he searched the gallery for the culprit, bringing a hush to the once bustling room.

Slowly, a hand rose from the crowd. "Kimmel Brickman, *Sporting News*. Hi, Trevor," said the reporter nervously. He appeared frozen, like a deer caught in the headlights. He took a deep breath and spoke. "I just thought you might have misspoken. I mean, your prediction was for a win this Saturday against Notre Dame, right? Not the entire season."

Trevor's eyes narrowed as he set his sights on the timid reporter. "Kimmel—did you say your name is Kimmel?" he asked mockingly, to the amusement of the entire room. "What the heck was your mama smoking when she named you?"

The reporter cleared his throat. "Well, my grandfather's name . . ."

"Look Kim, can I call you Kim?" interrupted Trevor. Then the smile returned to his face. "I'm telling you and everyone else in this room that, as sure as I'm standing here today, Trevor Hash will guarantee a second undefeated season and another national championship!"

The entire room broke out into hysterics, with nearly every reporter in the place trying desperately to ask questions of Trevor at the same time. Those who weren't vying for position were madly pecking away on their BlackBerrys, sending the news of Trevor's statements back to their publishers. The only one in the entire room who wasn't crazed was Trevor as he took in the madness he had just caused. Merely just a few simple words and he could completely bring down the house. The funny part about it was that they weren't just words to Trevor. He truly planned on never losing another football game—ever.

Trevor raised his hands with his palms facing the crowd in supplication. "Okay, okay, people, calm down, calm down," he said, laughing at the mayhem he had created. "Here's the deal, here's the deal," he said, as he regained control over the room. The place fell silent with everyone hanging on Trevor's next words. "Trevor Hash will win every game this season including the national championship. If Trevor Hash doesn't," he said smiling, "Trevor Hash will give his Heisman Trophy to Kimmel Brickman who can sell it on E-bay and take his family to the Bahamas for a month."

Once again the entire room was in an uproar. Was this actually happening? Did Trevor 'Handsome' Hash just guarantee an undefeated season and a national championship for the USC Trojans against his Heisman Trophy?

"What?" asked Kimmel, sounding as shocked as he appeared. "Why me? I mean . . . I wouldn't even . . ."

"You're right Kimmel, my man, what was Trevor Hash thinking?" he replied, with his cocky grin stretching from ear to ear. "Cancel that, cancel that, what the heck was Trevor Hash thinking?" he repeated, as the entire room waited in amazement to see what he would say next.

Trevor tapped his index finger on his lips and appeared to be thinking. Then, with a look of enlightenment on his face, he raised both hands in the air and pointed at the crowd. "Okay people, new deal, new deal!" His grin was even wider now. He was completely in control, and he was moving at a speed of 100 miles an hour with his hair on fire. He looked confident, strong and powerful. He was indeed a superstar, and he was about to make $85 million over the next six years to throw a football. "If Trevor Hash don't make good on his promise to deliver another undefeated season and another national championship, Trevor Hash will personally auction off his Heisman Trophy to the highest bidder and the proceeds will go to a charity to be chosen by the sexy Ms. Naomi Brown."

Once again the entire room spun out of control with questions being fired from every direction. Everyone was desperately trying to get Trevor's attention at the same time.

"Trevor, Trevor, will you have any input in choosing the charity?"

"Trevor, over here, *Football Weekly*. How much do you think the Heisman will go for?"

"Trevor, is it true that the trophy is at your grandmother's house in Missouri?"

Trevor laughed. "Whoa, whoa, people, one at a time," he said, appearing very pleased at the commotion he had just caused. "Let's give the first question to Ms. Brown," he said with a grin, waving a careless hand in her direction.

Trying to maintain her composure and put Trevor's arrogant, sexist comments aside, Naomi Brown stood and pointed her handheld tape recorder in the direction of the stage. "Okay, Handsome." she said, and then a slight smile appeared on her face. "I only have one question for you. She paused as her smile widened. "How will this affect your relationship with Lefty Shapiro and your contract to play for the San Diego Chargers next season?"

All eyes turned to Trevor for a response, and for the first time since the death of his parents, Trevor Hash appeared to lose his cool. "My what?" He said, practically stuttering over his words. He paused and looked at Rinaldi and Gilberti who appeared to be as shocked as he was. He looked back at Naomi Brown, who still had her recorder pointing at Trevor, and had the look of vindication all over her face. *What's the matter Handsome, cat got your tongue?* "How did you hear about that? That's not public knowledge," he retorted.

Immediately, the Rossi brothers sprang into action. The larger of the two brothers, Mike Rossi, grabbed Trevor and quickly pulled him from the podium, while his 6'2" smaller brother, Steven, grabbed the microphone. "That will be all for today. For further information please check Trevor's Web site. Thank you." And without wasting a second, the two men ushered Trevor off the stage and into the locker room.

Trevor was furious. "How the fuck do they know about that?" he screamed, as the three men burst into the empty locker room. "That wasn't supposed to go public 'til after the season!" he shouted, as he kicked over a full jug of Gatorade onto the carpeted floor.

"Welcome to the world of high-profile sports, kid," said Mike Rossi as his brother Steven began dialing Lefty's number on his cell.

"Fucking paparazzo!" mumbled Trevor, shaking his head in disgust as he took a seat on the bench in front of his locker, trying to calm himself.

"Yeah, Lefty, he just finished," replied the Rossi brother with the cell phone. "The kid did awesome as usual, guaranteed an undefeated season and another national championship."

Trevor could hear laughter coming through the cell phone. Obviously, Lefty Shapiro was pleased with the way Trevor had handled the press conference.

"Yeah, that's not all, boss. Said if he don't make good on the deal, he'd auction off the Heisman and give the money to some chick's charity."

Trevor could hear more laughing, this time much louder.

"Yeah, he's right here, hang on." The smaller Rossi brother walked up to Trevor and shoved the phone in his face. Trevor looked down at the man's huge hand. It was like a bear's paw. The phone looked completely lost wedged between his enormous fingers. "Here ya go, kid, he wants to speak to you."

Trevor took the phone and walked to the back of the locker room in the direction of the showers. When he was a safe distance away, he looked back at the Rossi brothers. Mike Rossi was in the process of demonstrating on his brother Steven the proper way to execute a choke hold. Trevor shook his head and decided to get a little farther away. When he was past the long row of showers, he placed the cell phone against his ear. "Yes, Mr. Shapiro?" he asked cautiously.

"Kid, I love it, I fucking love it!" came the booming voice of Lefty Shapiro through the small speaker on the cell phone.

Trevor peered around the corner and saw that the smaller Rossi did not appreciate the chokehold demonstration, and was now in a shoving match with his larger brother. "Thank you, Mr. Shapiro." A brief pause to build courage. "But somehow they know about our deal with the Chargers. I swear, Mr. Shapiro, I didn't . . . ."

"Kid, calm down. They don't know shit. Trust me, it's all speculation. It's what those fucking piranhas do best. They speculate."

"But one of the reporters said . . ."

"Look, kid, no one in this town knows nuttin' unless I want 'em to. Got it?"

"Sure, Mr. Shapiro. It's just that if my teammates find out that I'm thinking of . . ."

"Teammates?" More laughter. "Look, kid, this time next year they'll all be lining up to get on your yacht for a chance at an autograph, and that includes Coach Rinaldi and his sidekick, Chuck Gilberti, too."

There was a long silence as Trevor pondered the image of signing an autograph for Coach Rinaldi on his own yacht. Lefty knew exactly what Trevor was thinking. He'd had this same conversation many times before. He knew it was best to just stay silent and let the fantasy play out until the last autograph was signed and the boat was on its way to Bora Bora. Finally, Trevor spoke. "Okay, if you say so, Mr. Shapiro," he replied hesitantly.

"If I say so? Kid, I just got off the phone with Frank Audino."

Trevor's eyes widened. "Frank Audino? The guy who owns the Chargers?"

"Yeah," replied Lefty, stretching out the end of the word for effect. "The guy who owns the Chargers. They're talkin' signing bonus of seven figures, kid. As in six zeros!"

Trevor leaned back against the wall and slid to the ground. He needed to sit. "No joke?" he asked.

Lefty's tone was more deliberate now. "I never joke when it comes to a deal, kid. Never"

Trevor was flustered. "I didn't think . . . I mean . . . I . . . I'm not sure what to say, Mr. Shapiro."

"Don't say nuttin', kid. Just keep winning ballgames, and for chrissakes, stay healthy! We can't afford any injuries. Got it?"

Trevor nodded. "Yes sir, Mr. Shapiro. I will, sir."

"Oh yeah, and kid, I almost forgot, I got you a little something. It's with Mikey and Stevie."

Trevor leaned over as far as he could to see what was going on around the corner. Strangely, the Rossi brothers had vanished. *Maybe Mikey killed Stevie and was dumping the body somewhere.* "You didn't have to do that, Mr. Shapiro."

"Get used to it, Handsome; you're a superstar now!"

Trevor hung up the phone and made his way back to his locker. As he approached, he sensed something was not right. The Rossi brothers were standing side by side at the entrance to the locker room, and both men appeared angry.

Trevor turned his palms upwards. "What's up, fellas?" he asked cautiously.

"What's up? I'll tell ya what's up, bitch," said the larger Rossi brother. "We're tired of babysitting your black ass, that's what's up."

Trevor put his hands in front of him with his palms facing the two angry gangsters. "Whoa, guys! Look, I never asked for you to . . ."

Suddenly, the smaller man interrupted him. He appeared to be reaching for something inside his suit jacket. "You never asked, you never asked. Save it for the media, Heisman."

Trevor's brain was racing a thousand miles a minute. Were these guys serious, or were they just fucking with him? Maybe this was just some crazy hazing thing that all pro ballers go through when they finally make it big. Trevor was pretty sure he could take them one at a time, but together it was gonna be a tough fight.

Trevor took a step back and tilted his head sideways. "Come on, are you two fucking with me, or what?"

"Fucking with you? Does this look like we're just fucking with you," said the smaller man as he pulled out a gun.

"Holy shit," screamed Trevor, as he instinctively raised his hands above his head.

Suddenly, both men started laughing hysterically. "Ho . . . ly . . . fu . . . king shit, did you see the expression on his face, Stevie?" said the larger Rossi, who was laughing so hard he could barely get the words out.

Trevor felt his heart beating out of his chest as he looked back and forth between the two brothers. "What, you mean you're just fucking with me?" asked Trevor nervously, with his hands still raised high above his head.

"Yeah, kid, of course we're just fucking with ya," said Stevie as he placed the gun back in the holster and straightened out his suit jacket.

"And you can put your arms down, too," said Mikey, still laughing at Trevor's terrified expression. "You think we're gonna cap our meal ticket right here in the USC locker room? Wasssamatta witchu, kid?" More laughter.

Slowly, Trevor lowered his arms to his sides. "You motherfuckers," he said, shaking his head. Then suddenly a smile came to his face as he began to laugh at his own gullibility.

"Kid, if you could have seen your face."

Trevor took a deep breath and rubbed his hand on the back of his neck. "Yeah, yeah, very funny."

"Oh yeah, there was something Lefty wanted us to give you, Heisman," said Stevie.

"And don't worry, kid, it's not a bullet," added his brother.

"Yeah, what's that?" asked Trevor, sounding completely un-amused.

Both men smiled and then moved apart from one another revealing a beautiful blond woman, probably a model, with black lines painted under her eyes like a football player. She was completely naked except for a tight fitting Chargers jersey cut off just below her breasts and a pair of black panties.

She smiled. "Hi, Trevor, um I mean, hi, Handsome," she said, as she walked up to him and kissed him full on the lips. She looked back at the Rossi brothers, "I see where he gets his nickname." Then she turned back to Trevor. "And congrats on your 85 million dollar deal with San Diego."

Trevor took a step back. "How the fuck does everyone know about this but me?" he said, to no one in particular.

"Have fun, kid," said Stevie, as the two men exited the locker room.

"Yeah," replied Mikey. "And don't worry so much. No one's out to kill ya."

"Yet," interjected Stevie, as the sound of both men's laughter echoed throughout the hallway.

CHAPTER 6

Brooklyn Sims stepped off the elevator on the forty-fourth floor of the Century Tower Building and made her way down the marble corridor in the direction of the Shapiro Agency. She gazed at her diamond studded Chopard watch, a recent gift to herself in celebration of her latest blockbuster movie, *Miami Tan*, which grossed 60 six million in its opening weekend. So what if it cost more than a Porsche? She was worth it. Besides, she was now officially a superstar. In fact, she had been in such a good mood after reading her reviews that she had purchased a second watch along with a matching necklace for her girlfriend.

It was 4:15p.m., and for once Brooke was actually early for a meeting with Lefty. She looked down at her watch for a second time just to be sure. *Yup, 4:15. At least this time I won't have to listen to one of his 'time is money' speeches,* she thought as she approached the entrance. She hesitated for a moment, took a deep breath and exhaled slowly. She was angry; angry with herself for feeling as anxious as she did every time she had to meet with Lefty. After all, she was the superstar now. He worked for her, didn't he? So why did she feel this way? The answer was simple: because Lefty could end her career with a single phone call, and he made this apparent every chance he got. It was a power trip—one he enjoyed very much.

Brooke sighed as she began to trouble her bottom lip between her teeth. She could see her reflection in the glass doors staring back at her. She looked ravishing, truly beautiful. "Fuck him," she said, and a smile came to her face as she pushed open the doors and proceeded into the Shapiro Talent Agency. She walked up to the woman sitting at the receptionist station, but didn't recognize her. She was the fourth person sitting there this month. However, she was by far the prettiest. *Probably a model looking for a few extra bucks,* thought Brooke. *Beats waiting tables.*

Tyler Paige looked up from her computer screen and smiled. "Well hello there, Ms. Sims. We were expecting you," she said. "Oh, and congratulations on *Miami Tan*. I saw it this weekend, and I loved it!"

Brooke smiled back. "Please, it's Brooke. Call me Brooke, and thank you very much for seeing my movie." Then she looked at the nameplate on the front of the desk. "Tyler." She paused for a moment. "What a pretty name you have. Tyler Paige, I like that."

Brooklyn Sims was one of Tyler's favorite actresses and the only female client at the Shapiro Agency that Tyler liked. Although they had never formally met, Brooke's laid-back personality and reputation in the business preceded her. She was strikingly beautiful, with long auburn hair and captivating blue eyes. If anyone should have been a Hollywood diva, it was Brooklyn Sims, but she was quite the opposite. Always has a friendly hello and never too busy for an autograph. With a 66 million dollar opening weekend and points on the back end, Tyler wondered just how long that would last.

Tyler leaned forward in her chair and guided her hair behind her ears with her fingers as she reached for the phone. "I'll let him know you're here."

Brooke's smile widened. "I'm early," she said proudly.

Suddenly, a loud voice boomed through the tiny speaker on Tyler's phone, so loud that it startled both women. A single word erupted, sounding more like a demand than a question. "What!"

Tyler frowned. "Mr. Shapiro, Brooklyn Sims is here to see you."

There was a long silence as both women stared at the phone. "She's early!" Lefty barked, so loudly that it caused the speaker to rattle. "She'll have to wait." Then he hung up.

Brooke slumped.

Tyler replaced the phone on its cradle and stood to her feet. She looked at Brooke and grinned. "I swear to God, that guy gets PMS like a chick."

Brooke smiled. "You mean like a bitch, don't you?" she said, and then both women started to laugh.

Tyler walked to the front of her desk and gestured to the corner of the room. "You can wait for him right over there, if you like," she said.

The seating area at the Shapiro Agency was exquisite to say the least. It more than made up for the lack of furnishings in Lefty's office. The furniture, which consisted of a small love seat, a coffee table, two end tables and a small lamp, were all custom-made for Lefty by his personal friend Donatella Versace and cost more than most people pay for their entire home. The carpet was purchased at auction from Sotheby's during the Jacqueline Kennedy Onassis estate sale, and it seemed sinful to Tyler to allow anyone near it, let alone walk on it while chugging down their Starbucks. The whole arrangement was situated in a corner graced by floor-to-ceiling windows, which, on less smoggy days, had beautiful views of the Hollywood Hills.

Brooke nodded and made her way across the large room, but before she could step foot on the pricy carpet, the door to Lefty's office swung open.

"Well, well, Brooklyn Sims, on time for a change," cackled Lefty.

The sound of Lefty's voice brought Brooke to a sudden halt. She clenched her fists and mouthed the word, "Fuck." Slowly she turned to face him and forced a smile. "So nice to see you, too . . . Marty."

The comment made Tyler chuckle. Lefty shot her a look and receded back into his office. Still smiling, she looked up at Brooke. "Mr. Shapiro will see you now."

Brooke gave her a wink and proceeded into Lefty's office. She looked around and shook her head. "Ya think you could invest in some furniture?"

Lefty ignored the comment and fell back into his chair. The distinct sound of escaping air echoed throughout the cavernous room as the chair struggled to support his weight. It sounded like a deflating balloon, and it made Brooke smile. "Did you see this weekend's numbers? he asked, sliding a copy of *Variety* across his desk. On the cover was a picture of Brooke and her co-star in a scene from her movie. The headline read, *Miami Tan Opens at Record High!*

Brooke gazed down at the cover. Her heart raced and she wanted to scream for joy. But she would never let on, especially in front of Lefty. That was what he wanted, just another reason to show how indebted she was to him. *Controlling prick!* "I may have heard something about this," she said as she picked up the magazine and read the headline over and over again in her head.

Lefty let out a sarcastic laugh. "Yeah right, kid." He leaned back in his seat and propped his feet up on his cluttered desktop. The chair hissed and groaned and looked as if it was about ready to collapse at any moment. "You know, with the points I got you on the back end of this deal, you could be looking at 50 mil."

Yes, well maybe I could hike up my skirt and bend over your desk to repay you. Or maybe the 20 percent you get for sitting on your fat ass should be enough. Brooke bit her lip and stayed silent.

Suddenly, a serious look came over Lefty's face. His voice was more deliberate now. "But kid, listen to me," he said, as his feet dropped to the floor and he slid his chair into his desk. "We need to preserve your pure image."

Brooke tilted her head sideways. "I don't understand, Mr. Shapiro."

"Your image, kid. Your image. It's what got you the big bucks in this flick. It's untarnished and it's got to stay that way."

Brooke looked confused. "I still don't know what you're talking about Mr. Sh . . . ."

"I'm talkin' about no late-night parties, no club-hopping and definitely no drugs!" Lefty paused and leaned into his desk as far as his stomach would allow. He could see he wasn't getting through. "Look, kid, ya gotta think Disney Channel."

Brooke shook her head. "But Mr. Shapiro, I don't do any . . ."

Lefty raised the palm of his hand and waved it at Brooke. "Disney Channel, kid. That means no slutty, porn star, stripper girlfriend either."

Brooke gasped in exasperation. "Mr. Shapiro, I don't see what my private life has to do with anything."

Lefty let out another sarcastic laugh, this one louder than the first. "Brooke baby, you're a superstar now. You don't have a private life anymore."

Brooke's head sunk. She was speechless.

Lefty stood and walked around to the front of his desk. He put a hand on Brooke's shoulder. "Look, kid, no one wants Brooklyn Sims to be a carpet muncher." He paused and led her to the door. "Not yet anyway. Give it a few years. Get yourself a foothold in this town and then you can pull an Ellen and come out of the closet."

Brooke sighed. *Maybe he was right. After all, he did get her to where she was today and she certainly didn't want to lose that.* She opened the door and turned to face him. "Okay, Mr. Shapiro, anything you say."

Lefty smiled. "Oh and kid, before I forget," he said, as he pulled a business card from his pocket and handed it to Brooke. "You have a 5:30 p.m. consultation with Dr. Axelrod. He's the best nose man in town."

Brooke looked at the card and then back up at Lefty. "A plastic surgeon?"

Lefty nodded. "Like I said, think Disney, kid. Young faces and button noses."

"But, Mr. Shapiro, I'm only 22."

Lefty turned and started walking back to his desk. "In this town you're over the hill at 21, kid."

Brooke looked back down at the card. She wanted to cry. Once again she forced a smile. "Anything you say, Mr. Shapiro."

CHAPTER 7

SKYLER DAWN DROVE HER candy-apple red Mercedes SL500 convertible to the bottom of the long, cobblestone driveway leading to Brooke's home in the Hollywood Hills. It was nearly 5:00 p.m., and with the sun now dangling low on the horizon, Skyler could feel the last of the day's warmth shining on her face. Slowly, she brought the car to a halt. There was a wrought-iron fence supported by two large stone pillars on either side of the driveway. Leaning over her door, Skyler punched a 4-digit code into the security panel affixed to one of the pillars.

Slowly, the gates swung open revealing a long, winding road lined with rows of royal palms, leading to a large stone mansion. A light evening breeze caused the tops of the palms to rustle against the twilight sky. The look was majestic. Once the gates were fully opened, Skyler shifted the sports car into gear, floored the accelerator, and sped up to the house.

Sky Dawn was a hooker; a very, very expensive hooker. In the business, girls like her were referred to as high-priced escorts, but it all meant the same thing—sex for money. In fact, a night with Sky would run you 10 grand and the whole weekend closer to 50. Once some sheik from Dubai had paid Skyler's agency a half million dollars for Sky to spend a week with his son for his 18th birthday. Even with the agency taking their cut, Sky had made more money in one week than some people make in a lifetime. Except all Sky had to do was sun herself on the Persian Gulf, drink umbrella drinks and de-virginize the sheik's kid. At 21, Skyler Dawn had it all figured out.

Skyler brought the Benz to a screeching stop in front of a large building that housed a long row of garage doors. There were six wooden bays in all, and their rustic appearance resembled vintage carriage doors on the side of an old barn. The structure formed a right angle with the main home, and a Spanish cedar pergola, completely covered by flowering rose vines, joined the buildings. Along the rooflines, around the window frames and down the sides of both structures grew dark green ivy. The look was vintage Hollywood.

In front of both buildings was a cobblestone courtyard with a decorative fountain at its center. Inlaid in the cobblestones, by the cedar pergola, were the initials CGCL. At one time the estate had belonged to Clark Gable and Carole Lombard. Gable had named the mansion "Tara," after Scarlett O'Hara's plantation in *Gone With the Wind*, and above one of the carriage doors he had hung a hand carved, wooden sign bearing that name.

Sky angled the rearview mirror so that she could see her reflection. After applying a fresh coat of lip gloss, she ran her fingers through her strawberry blond hair and smiled at her reflection. Pleased with the effect, she repositioned the mirror and grabbed her Dolce & Gabbana purse from the passenger side seat and a leather weekender from the back. Throwing the strap over her shoulder she exited the car and headed toward the house. Skyler stopped momentarily in front of two large, stained-glass doors that sat majestically atop a grand staircase at the entrance to the home. She fumbled through the bag in search of her set of house keys. Nothing. Then she undid the zipper in the side of her purse, but as she reached in, felt a sharp pain. "Fuck!" she exclaimed, as she quickly extracted her hand and brought it to her face. "Motherfucker!" she shouted, as she examined a hairline fracture along one or her french-manicured fingernails. With a huff, she removed the leather strap from her shoulder and threw her bag to the ground. It slammed hard against the base of the door causing it to gently swing open. Sky let out a condescending chuckle and shook her head. "Brooke, how many times do I have to remind you?" she muttered as she picked up her bag, repositioned the strap over her shoulder and entered the house. The alarm panel was flashing the words, *alarm disengaged* in bright red letters. Skyler shook her head again, dropped her bag beside a rattan chair that was nestled along one of the walls in the entrance, and made her way into the kitchen. She walked directly to the Sub Zero refrigerator, yanked open the freezer door, and pulled out a bottle of Grey Goose Vodka. She let out a sigh. "God, I need a drink," she said, as she filled a glass halfway, brought it to her mouth, and chugged down the ice-cold vodka in a single gulp. She took a deep breath and exhaled slowly. The warmth of the alcohol inside her felt comforting. She refilled the glass, this time full up, placed the bottle back in the freezer and headed in the direction of the master bath for a long, warm soak. As she made her way out of the kitchen she gazed out the sliding glass doors onto the patio. There was a full moon that was beginning to show in the twilight sky and reflecting off the pool, causing it to sparkle. Skyler tilted her head, considering. *Change in plans.*

She walked up to the glass doors and gazed out at the pool and spa. They looked inviting. She reached over to a small control panel beside one of the doors, raised the plastic cover and depressed a small button with the image of a light bulb on it. Suddenly, the pool and spa lit up the patio with an aquamarine glow. Skyler smiled and took a big sip from her glass. The alcohol was beginning to take effect. Setting the spa temperature to 103 degrees, she grabbed her purse and made her way out to the pool. It was a beautiful fall night.

Skyler walked up to a large rattan table situated next to the spa. The top of the table was covered in glass and had a multi-colored umbrella protruding through its center. She placed her drink down on the surface and kicked off her shoes. The pavement felt cool on the bottom of her feet as she curled her toes inward. She reached into her purse and took out a small glass vial and a thin straw. The vial was filled with a white powder. *Cocaine.* She held it up against the moonlight and frowned. "That won't do," she said, as she pulled her BlackBerry from her purse and typed a note to her drug dealer. *Desi, I'm staying with Brooke for the weekend, and am in desperate need of some party favors, perhaps an eight-ball? Thanks, sweetie. Sky.*

Emptying the vial onto the table, Skyler used her pinky to arrange the powder into a neat line. That done, she brought the straw to her nostril, leaned over, and snorted the coke deep into her lungs. She closed her eyes and slowly tilted her head back, tweaking the side of her nose with her fingers. She could feel her pulse begin to race as the drug began to take control of her brain. Suddenly, her PDA began to vibrate causing it to dance along the glass table. Skyler opened her eyes and smiled. "Wow, Desi. That was quick. Even for you," she said, as she grabbed her PDA and looked down at the screen. But to her surprise the e-mail was from Brooke. *Sky, I'm going to be about an hour late. My fucking agent set up some ridiculous meeting with a plastic surgeon. Sorry, baby. I love you. Brooke.*

Skyler let out a scornful laugh. "Don't sound so upset, lover. I had to pay 15 thousand for my tits. You're getting yours done for free," she murmured, as she slid the spaghetti straps off her shoulders and let her skimpy dress fall to the floor. She then tossed the PDA onto a nearby chaise lounge, grabbed her iPod from her purse, and with a tiny earbud in each ear, cautiously stepped into the steaming spa. The water was hot and it made her feet tingle. Slowly, she submerged her naked body into the bubbling water and it gave her goose bumps. "Mmmm, that's so nice," she cooed, as she turned on her iPod and increased the volume as loud as it would go.

So loud, in fact, that she didn't hear The Artist as he slid open the glass doors, walked out onto the stone patio, and positioned himself directly behind her. He was carrying a large canvas bag that he set down on the ground, merely inches from her head. He knelt down beside the bag, undid the long metal zipper and pulled out a small golden statue. It was an exact replica of an Oscar award, and carved into the base of the statue, were three words—Shapiro Talent Agency.

The Artist's face was void of all expression, completely emotionless. He could feel the heat as it rose from the turbulent water, and he could hear the muffled sound of music being emitted from the tiny buds nestled in Skyler's ears. He leaned forward and brought his nose to the back of her neck, took in her scent and smiled sadistically. He then carefully hid the small statue under one of the plantings beside the spa and reached back into the satchel. He was desperately fighting to control the voices in his head that seemed to be screaming at him now. He took a deep breath and pulled out a three-foot long machete, the kind an explorer would use to hack down the thick brush of an overgrown jungle. He grasped the wooden handle tightly, slowly stood to his feet, and raised the machete high over his shoulder like a baseball player readying himself for the next pitch. "Goodbye, Brooke," he uttered through clenched teeth as he violently swung the machete down with such force that the blade sliced through Skyler's neck, causing her body to lurch forward into the hot tub, while her decapitated head flew from her shoulders and splashed into the adjoining swimming pool. Skyler Dawn was dead.

CHAPTER 8

JAKE GAZED OUT THE SMALL WINDOW of the Gulfstream G5 as the jet slowly taxied along the tarmac in the direction of a private aviation hangar at LAX. He could see a multitude of runways lined with flickering lights that appeared to run endlessly into the distance. It was starting to drizzle, and small beads of water began to form and trickle down the outside of the jet's window. He sighed and pulled down the plastic shade. "I can't believe I'm back in fucking LA," he mumbled to himself, as he brought his hand to his face and traced his fingers along a two-inch scar on his left cheek; a souvenir from the Paramount case. He looked down at his watch and frowned. It was almost midnight.

Unfortunately, whoever had sent the e-mail had followed through on the threat. At 9 PM, West Coast time, the LAPD had received an anonymous phone call originating from a house in an exclusive section of the Hollywood Hills. The male caller reported a homicide; the brutal decapitation of a young woman.

Jake reached over and grabbed his BlackBerry from the adjoining seat. He scrolled through a long, detailed e-mail Director Robbins had sent regarding the murder and what the FBI knew so far. *Not much.* There were attached photos of the crime scene that revealed gruesome images of a headless body floating in a blood-filled hot tub. Jake shook his head. *Whoever did this had some serious rage issues.*

He then toggled to an e-mail sent from the bureau's IT Department Chief, Michael Jarvis.

Jarvis had recently been promoted to an executive position at the FBI and had been given "level one" clearance because of his efforts in helping solve the Paramount case. That meant he had access to any and all classified material, from inter-office e-mails to top secret documents, and it also meant that he reported directly to Jake and Director Robbins. Indeed, Paramount had been a career maker for some and a career breaker for others.

> *To: Deputy Director Chase*
> *From: Michael Jarvis, CTO*
> *Re: LA Homicide*
>
> *Jake,*
> *I was able to trace the e-mail sent to your BlackBerry to a student account at USC. The sender probably snatched it from an unsuspecting student. We are looking into that now. Also, the sender did not hack into the bureau's system. Somehow he got hold of your personal e-mail account.*
>
> *Give me a few days. I'll have more.*
>
> *Jarvis*

Just then, there was a loud whining sound coming from the jet engines as the plane came to a stop. The sudden noise startled Jake. He looked up from his BlackBerry in the direction of the cockpit door. The flight attendant caught his eye and smiled reassuringly as she unbuckled her safety belt. She then rose from her seat and walked down the aisle in Jake's direction. "Is there anything I can get for you, Mr. Chase?"

Jake shook his head. "I'm fine," he replied, as he unclasped his belt and stood up. He raised his arms above his head and arched his back in a big stretch. He could hear crackling noises coming from his vertebrae. As he made his way to the front of the aircraft, he noticed what appeared to be a myriad of flashing lights coming from the tarmac. He leaned over and looked out of the windows near the front of the jet. "Fuck!" he shouted, so loud it made the flight attendant jump.

"What's wrong, Mr. Chase?" asked the captain, who quickly emerged from the cockpit. "Is everything okay?"

Jake had purposefully taken Jack's private Gulfstream to avoid media attention. After Paramount, Jake had become a celebrity, and he hated every minute of it. Jake Chase had become a household name and he was stalked by the paparazzi day and night. Even his appointment to Deputy Director of the FBI was a media frenzy with news vans, reporters and camera crews camped out in front of Quantico for days. One tabloid had even mistakenly referred to Jake as one of America's most eligible bachelors. *Diane loved that one.* Only recently had things begun to quiet down, but now it was starting all over again. He slammed down the shade and turned to face the pilot and pointed an angry finger in his direction. "Did you tip them off, Chuck?"

The captain turned his palms to Jake. "Whoa, hang on a minute. I've been flying for you and Diane for how many years now?" He paused. "And I was friends with old Jack, God rest his soul, since before my days in the Navy." He slowly returned his hands to his sides and took a breath.

Jake looked back and forth between the pilot and the flight attendant. "Then how the fuck do they know we're here, Chuck?"

The captain motioned to the flight attendant. "Corinne, please lower the hatch and prepare for deplaning." He then stepped closer to Jake and placed a hand on his shoulder. "Look, son, these guys are piranhas, scum of the earth, and every private aviation pilot knows that. No one's gonna sell out to them, Jake, especially not me." He paused, and then took his hand off Jake's shoulder. "These guys monitor live air traffic on two-way radios from their homes." He paused again, this time longer. "Christ, you can even listen in on flight deck conversations on the internet if you wanted to."

Jake narrowed his eyes. He appeared much calmer now. "So what are you saying?"

The captain reached into one of the storage compartments, took out Jake's blazer and garment bag, and handed them over. "What I'm saying, Deputy Director, is that these scumbags keep updated lists of VIPs and their private jet tail-markers. You know, KBR 660—Paris Hilton, TRU 590-Donald Trump, STH . . . well, you get the picture."

Jake stayed silent. What he was hearing didn't surprise him a bit.

The captain continued. "We have to call in our markers on approach, and if these guys like what they hear, they are on the tarmac before our wheels are down."

Jake sighed. "So what you're saying, Chuck, is that I've made the list?"

Corinne let out a slight chuckle as she lowered the hatch and peered out onto the tarmac. "Judging by the number of paparazzi out there, I'd say you're at the top of the list, Deputy Director."

CHAPTER 9

THE WROUGHT-IRON GATES that once appeared so majestic at the foot of the long driveway leading to the Sims estate were now crudely held open by two large concrete blocks. There was a patrol car parked across the street, and its lights cast red and blue dancing shadows onto the stone pillars where two uniformed police officers laughed and smoked cigarettes.

Jake pulled up to the patrolmen and rolled down the car window. Simultaneously, both officers stopped what they were doing and stared at him through the open window. They appeared annoyed as they each took a final drag on their cigarettes and flung them onto the cobblestone driveway.

Jake retrieved his wallet from his back pocket but before he could get to his ID, the two men were shinning flashlights in his face.

"Hey, wanna turn this thing around," demanded one of the officers, as he abruptly tapped his flashlight on the hood of the car then directed the light back down the road.

"Yeah, this is a crime scene, buddy. Move it along," interjected the other officer.

Jake stayed silent and handed over his credentials.

The two men appeared confused as one of them reached in and took the ID from Jake. Suddenly, his eyes widened. "Holy shit! He's Jake Chase," exclaimed the officer holding Jake's credentials up to his flashlight-wielding sidekick. Then he paused and looked back down into the car nervously. "You're Jake Chase."

Jake sighed. "Yesss," he replied in frustration, drawing out the *s* through clenched teeth. "I'm Jake Chase," he repeated, as he reached to retrieve his identification. Then he forced a smile "May I proceed, officers?"

"Certainly, Mr. Chase, right this way," said one of the officers, shining his flashlight up the long driveway.

Jake then sped up to the house and pulled in behind a row of assorted emergency vehicles: LAPD, Los Angeles Fire and the Los Angeles Medical Examiner were all represented in full force, and, of course, the entire place was bustling with media activity. News vans, camera crews, reporters and photographers were scattered about the front of the home, all hoping to get the early scoop on what many were referring to as the most brutal slaying since the Charles Manson murders. There was a long row of yellow police tape cordoning off a section for news media personnel, which for the most part was being ignored. The two uniformed officers assigned to crowd control were busy posing for a photograph in front of Clark Gable's hand-carved "Tara" sign. The rain had now turned to a slight mist and everything was enveloped in a layer of dampness.

Jake shook his head in amazement. He stepped out of the car, turned up the collar on his blazer and headed quickly in the direction of the front door.

Suddenly, one of the reporters spotted him. "Hey, it's Jake Chase," she shouted, as she hurried toward him with her cameraman in tow. "Jake, Dede Ericksen, *LA*

Buzz". She then turned to the cameraman and signaled for him to start recording. "Jake, what the heck are the Feds doing investigating a Los Angeles homicide?" She asked excitedly, angling her microphone towards his face.

Jake continued forward. In fact, he picked up the pace and made a beeline for the front door. Unfortunately, before he could get into the house, he was encircled by a throng of reporters, all shouting questions and pointing microphones in his face.

"Hi, Jake, Allison Bishop, *Hollywood Daily*. Does the FBI have any leads on the killer?"

"Jake, has the FBI made any progress on tracking down Ken Devasher?" shouted another voice.

"Jake, Dede Ericksen again. How's Diane feeling? Have you found out the sex of the twins?"

Suddenly, the front door burst open and a giant hand grabbed Jake's shoulder and pulled him backwards into the house. Instinctively, Jake grabbed the man's hand and spun him around, twisting his arm behind his back. With his free hand Jake then grabbed the huge assailant by the back of his neck and forced him against the wall, face first. *Slam!*

With his mouth pressed tightly against the wall the large man let out a hearty laugh. Then he spoke. "I read in *People Magazine* that you were quick on your feet, Deputy Director."

Jake shook his head as he released his grip on the man's arm and head. *I really can't believe I'm back in fucking LA.*

Slowly, the man turned to face Jake, brushed off his already wrinkled suit and extended his hand. His grip was firm and his smile genuinely friendly. "Nails

Krycerick, Chief Detective, LA homicide." His voice sounded hoarse. "Director Robbins and I are old friends. He filled me in about the e-mail and asked that I act as your liaison with LAPD." Then he paused. His voice was lower now. "Said there was a lot of dick-measuring going on between police and the Feds during Paramount."

Jake's jaw tightened. "Yeah, well I'll tell ya what. You boys stay out of my way, and I'll stay out of yours. Got that?"

Chief Krycerick grinned. "Still completely pissed off about how LAPD handled Paramount, huh Deputy Director? I read that one in *Esquire Magazine*."

Jake gave a slight smile. "Did you say Nails?"

The detective shrugged his shoulders. "Yeah, it's actually Eddie, Eddie Krycerick, but all these guys call me Nails," he said, gesturing with his thumb to a group of police officers who were busy dusting the living room and kitchen for prints.

Chief Detective Eddie "Nails" Krycerick had been on the job for more than 20 years, and, although in his late 40's, he had the appearance of a much younger man. He stood nearly 6'5" and was apparently no stranger to the gym, with broad shoulders and muscular arms. He wore his dirty blond hair combed back off his face, and looked like Nick Nolte in the movie *48 Hours*.

"Right this way, Deputy Director" said Detective Krycerick and he led Jake through the bustling house in the direction of the swimming pool. He let out a slight chuckle. "You know, you really gottta watch out for those paparazzi," he said, as the two men made their way through the living room. "Trust me, I know. I used to be married to one of them."

Jake reached into his blazer pocket and took out a pair of latex gloves. He slid one over each hand and reached for the sliding glass doors leading out to the patio. Before he could get the door open he was distracted by a loud commotion coming from the next room.

"I got a clean one! I got a clean print!" yelled Officer Jeff Lewis, who had been dusting for prints in the kitchen. Suddenly, the house fell quiet. All eyes were now looking through the stone archway that joined the two rooms as Officer Lewis examined a detailed fingerprint on a clear piece of print-lifting tape. He slid a pair of magnifying glasses onto the bridge of his nose and held the tape up against the bright kitchen light. "Yup, it's clean and it doesn't belong to Ms. Sims or the vic."

Jake and Detective Krycerick exchanged glances. "Okay, people, back to work," ordered Krycerick as he and Jake made their way into the kitchen. Officer Lewis was now in the process of placing the fingerprint tape into a large evidence baggie with a pair of tweezers.

Jake approached the man and read the officer's badge. "What have you found, Officer Lewis?" he asked. His voice was deliberate.

The policeman looked up at Jake over the top of the magnifiers, which were still resting on the bridge of his nose, and smiled. "I lifted this print off the kitchen phone," he replied, as he placed the tweezers down on the countertop and sealed the top of the evidence baggie. He examined the print again. "Judging by the oil content, it's extremely fresh, like as in the last three or four hours fresh. And it's a negative match on Brooklyn Sims or Ichabod out in the pool," he said, nodding in the direction of the murder scene.

Chief Krycerick grinned. "The headless horseman was a guy, genius." He paused. "And so was Ichabod Crane for that matter." He then looked out the window at Skyler's naked body being extracted from the hot tub by two forensic technicians from the Medical Examiner's Office. "You might wanna take an anatomy course, Jeff."

"Yeah, yeah, guy, girl. You want I should get this over to forensics, Nails?"

Chief Krycerick leaned over and took the baggie from his colleague. He then reached into his suit pocket and removed an old pair of bifocals. Jake noticed that one arm was held in place by silver-colored duct tape and the right lens was cracked. He allowed himself a slight smile.

The chief then held the print against the light. His eyes narrowed in deep concentration. "Now, where did you come from little fella?" he muttered to himself, as he examined the print from various angles. He then pulled out a small notepad and pencil and scribbled down some notes. When he was done, he handed the baggie to Jake. "What do you think, Deputy Director?"

Officer Lewis' eyes widened. "Whoa!" he exclaimed. "I knew I recognized you," he said, pointing a finger at Jake. "You're that FBI guy!"

Jake ignored the comment as he examined the print. He walked to the kitchen phone, lifted it from the cradle, and compared it side by side with the bagged evidence. He then held the receiver to his nose and took a whiff.

Officer Lewis looked over at Chief Krycerick and shrugged his shoulders. "Nails, what the heck are the Fibbies doing investigating an LA homicide?"

The Chief turned up the palms of his hands. "Don't ask me, I was . . . ."

Suddenly, the sound of a woman screaming came from the next room. Once again Jake and Krycerick shot each other a look that sent both men running in the direction of the screaming woman.

Two female officers in front of the glass doors leading to the murder scene were restraining Brooklyn Sims. She was hysterical, with her arms and legs flailing to break free. "No, no, please no!" she screamed, and then fell to her knees and began keening.

Jake immediately tugged hard on a cord beside the doors, releasing a set of dark blinds to block the gruesome view of Brooke's blood-filled pool and her girlfriend's headless body. He then knelt beside the sobbing woman and placed a hand gently on her shoulder. He looked up at the two female officers. "We'll be fine."

"Certainly, Deputy Director," they both replied in unison.

Krycerick pulled back the blinds and opened one of the glass doors. Immediately, Jake could hear the activity coming from outside.

The chief then squeezed his body out onto the stone patio. "Whenever you're ready, Jake," he said and closed the door behind him, leaving the room silent.

Jake turned to Brooke. His hand was still resting on her shoulder. "Ms. Sims, my name is Jake Chase."

Brooke didn't look up. "I know who you are." She then brushed away his hand as she stood to her feet. She was no longer crying but was still visibly upset.

Jake sighed. "Well, then you know that I can help you," he said, as he slowly stood and gestured toward the couch with an open hand. "Please," he said, smiling sympathetically.

Brooke reached into her purse and pulled out a wad of tissues. With trembling hands, she wiped away the smeared mascara below her watery eyes. "Mr. Chase, I don't understand what the FBI has to do with Sky." She started to cry again as she quickly brought the tissues to her face. "I mean, I know she wasn't the nicest person . . . and the people she hung out with . . ." Her voice trailed off into light sobs.

Jake put his arm around Brooke's shoulder and led her to the couch. "Please, Ms. Sims, it's Jake, and if you would have a seat, I will explain everything."

Brooke took a deep breath and fell back into the sofa. Her hair flopped into her face and Jake noticed that under the halogen spots, it appeared to have a strawberry glow to it. She let out a sad sigh as she pushed it from her face, revealing the bluest eyes Jake had ever seen. She began to trouble her bottom lip between her teeth again. A nervous habit she had developed when she had come to LA. "I need a fucking cigarette. I don't suppose you smoke, do ya, Jake?"

Jake smiled as he sat down across from her. "Look, Ms. Sims . . ."

"It's Brooklyn." She paused. "Or Brooke . . . whichever," she said, dabbing the clump of tissues below each nostril.

Jake leaned forward in his seat and rested his elbows on his knees. His voice was more deliberate now. "Listen, Brooke, I have reason to believe that your life may be in danger. I don't think Skyler was who the killer was after."

Brooke stopped what she was doing. She appeared confused. "I don't understand. Who would want to hurt me?" She paused and thought for a moment, then, once again, began to gnaw on her lip, more ferociously now. "I mean, Sky was the one with all of the enemies, not me."

Jake leaned in even closer. "I understand that but . . ."

Brooke shook her head. She had a distant look in her eyes. "No, Sky was the dangerous one. Go talk to her fucking pimp or that goddamn junkie drug dealer. I'm sure they'll have some answers."

Jake took a deep breath and exhaled through closed lips. "All the same, I think it would be best if you didn't stay . . ."

Brooke let out a sarcastic laugh. "You want me to leave my home?" She huffed. "Now you listen . . . Jake. Skyler Dawn was bad news. Everyone in town knew that." She began slowly shaking her head side to side. "They all warned me about her and I guess I just should have listened."

Brooke then stood to her feet. She appeared agitated. "Does anyone have a goddamn cigarette!"

Suddenly, the glass door slid open and Chief Krycerick peered in from behind the blinds. "Jake, there's someone I think you should meet."

Jake stood to his feet. He reached into his blazer pocket, took out a card and handed it to Brooke. "Be sure to leave the names and phone numbers of Skyler's associates with one of the detectives," he said. "My cell number is on the back, and I'll be staying at the Beverly Hills Hotel." Brooke took the card from Jake and stared down at it momentarily. She then looked up at him. It was the first time that she had actually looked directly at him. An approving smile came to her face. "I thought you'd be older, Deputy Director." She then turned and walked towards her bedroom, but then stopped and looked over her shoulder. "You know, Jake, for the guy who saved Paramount, you sure don't know a lot about Hollywood." She disappeared around the corner.

Jake shook his head in amazement. "I really can't believe I'm back in fucking LA," he muttered under his breath, as he pulled the latex gloves back onto his hands and made his way out onto the stone patio.

The crime scene was busy with emergency personnel, mostly forensic technicians from the Los Angeles Medical Examiner's Office, a few plainclothes detectives, and, of course, Nails Krycerick, calling all the shots. Skyler's corpse was now lying on a stretcher, sealed in a thick, black plastic body bag. A few of the medical technicians were standing beside the stretcher and were deep in discussion about Kobe Bryant and the Lakers.

Jake walked in the direction of the pool. It was narrow and much smaller than he had imagined; built for swimming laps, one swimmer at a time. He approached the edge and looked down at the water, which was now a dark shade of red. The effect was eerie. "And I will strike the water and it shall be turned to blood," he observed.

One of the detectives overheard him and let out a chuckle. He squinted his eyes, considering, then pointed a finger at Jake. "One of the deadly sins, right, Deputy Director?"

"No!" interrupted Chief Krycerick, as he walked up to the pool and stood beside Jake. He looked down at the water. "It's one of the ten plagues of Egypt, numb-nuts."

The detective appeared confused.

"The first plague actually," mumbled Krycerick, still looking down at the blood-red water. "I will strike the water that is in the Nile with the staff that is in my hand, and it shall be turned to blood. Exodus 7:17." The Chief looked up at Jake and shrugged his shoulders. "Catholic school."

Just then, an attractive woman in her mid. 40's approached the two men. She was wearing a blue windbreaker with the words LA Medical Examiner's Office written across the back in large yellow letters. She had on the same latex gloves as everyone else, except hers were covered in dried blood. "So, which one of you guys is the Pharaoh?" she asked, and then gave Chief Krycerick a wink. "Hey, Nails," she said, with a friendly smile.

Chief Krycerick gave a nod. "Dr. Bonina, I'd like you to meet . . ."

"Deputy Director Chase," she said, finishing his sentence. She peeled off a glove and extended her hand. "Doctor Andrea Bonina, Los Angeles Medical Examiner. I've read a lot about you, Deputy Director."

Jake slipped off a glove and took the woman's hand. He was amazed at how soft her hands were, yet how firm her grip was. "Nice to meet you, Doctor," he said, as he glanced over her shoulder and watched the team of medical technicians wheel the stretcher, with Skyler's body through the glass doors and into the house. He then looked back down at the woman. "Any clues, Doctor?"

Dr. Bonina let go of Jake's hand and the expression on her face suddenly changed. Her confident look had become sullen, frightened even. She shook her head and looked back down at the blood-filled pool. "Deputy Director, I haven't seen anything this violent this since the O.J. Simpson case. Pure rage." She then reached into her pocket, pulled out a small note pad and handed it to Jake. "Here are my notes. If you can't read my chicken scratch, Dr. Krycerick can translate for you."

Jake looked at the Chief and raised his eyebrows. "Dr. Krycerick?"

Dr. Bonina smiled. "Yes," she replied. She then looked at the Chief and grinned. "You didn't tell him, Nails?"

The Chief let out a groan. "What are ya doin', Andrea?"

She then looked back at Jake. "Once upon a time, old Nails and I suffered through Cornell Medical School together." She chuckled. "If memory serves, he graduated magna cum laude, too."

"Summa cum laude," muttered Krycerick under his breath. "But who's counting?"

Dr. Bonina laughed. "Okay, gentlemen, let me get back to work." She handed her card to Jake. "If my office can be of any assistance, Deputy Director . . ." she said, as she made her way into the house.

Jake looked down at the pad she had given him. More dried blood. He flipped to the first page and began to read Dr. Bonina's hand-written notes. His eyes burned and he was finding it difficult to concentrate. He glanced down at his watch: 4:00 a.m. He brought his hand to the back of his neck and tried to squeeze out some of the knots, but it was no use. He returned to the journal:

October 24, 2009—2:13AM
Skyler Dawn—female
Cause of death: decapitation
Approximate time of death: unknown
Approximate age: 20

Chief Krycerick clucked his tongue and shook his head disapprovingly as he scrolled through Skyler's BlackBerry. "Our vic certainly wasn't pure in thought or word," he said, shaking his head more deliberately now.

Jake continued to read:
Approximate height: 5'7"
Approximate weight: 115lbs
Known profession: stripper/prostitute

Jake closed the journal. He brought the palms of his hands to his bloodshot eyes and began rubbing them in a small circular motion. "Or deed," he said.

Suddenly, Chief Krycerick's eyes widened. "Hey Jake, have a look at this," he said, handing over the BlackBerry.

Jake looked down at the screen and scrolled through the text. It was the e-mail that Skyler had sent to her drug dealer earlier that evening and it was time-stamped 7:42 p.m. "Well, we can assume she was still breathing when she sent this," he said. "Now we can establish a timeline."

Krycerick nodded at Jake. "You think this Desi DiSisto is our man?"

Jake shook his head. "No, but I think you'll find Mr. DiSisto's prints match the ones we found all over that phone." Jake rubbed his forehead then continued. "And, Nails . . ."

Chief Krycerick grinned.

"I'll bet you a beer he wears cheap cologne."

CHAPTER 10

IT WAS NEARLY 7:00 A.M. ON SATURDAY MORNING by the time The Artist finally awoke. He was still fully clothed and was sprawled out on the floor of the single-room efficiency he rented on Sunset Boulevard. His head was throbbing, and there was loud music coming through the wall from the room next door. Slowly, he managed to pull himself into a sitting position, using a tattered old dresser for support. He felt nauseous and everything around him seemed to be spinning in slow motion. He took a deep breath and reached for a package of Marlboro Lights from the coffee table. He removed one of the cigarettes and placed it between his lips. He stood on unsteady feet and made his way to the stove in the small kitchenette. Twice he had to catch his balance to prevent himself from falling. He was completely out of sorts, even more so than usual. Once in the kitchen, he turned on the gas, leaned forward, and brought the cigarette to the open flame. He inhaled deeply, allowing the smoke and nicotine to fill his lungs.

He then made his way back into the living area and began searching for some sign that she had actually been there with him last night; possibly an article of clothing left behind in the mad rush to escape. *Nothing*.

He was getting worse by the day and was now experiencing great difficulty in distinguishing reality from fantasy. He paused and thought for a long moment, then grabbed his pillow and brought it to his face. He shut his eyes so tightly that his brow rippled as he sought to recall the events of the past 12 hours. He breathed in through his mouth and nose and could smell her odor lingering on the pillowcase. Her scent was unmistakable. She had been there with him, in his room last night, and they had fucked each other's brains out. *Yes, he was certain of it.*

The Artist opened his eyes and smiled. He took a long drag on his cigarette and then exhaled a stream of smoke that crashed angrily into the wall and dissipated into the already stale room. He let out a crude cackle as he fell back into the tattered sofa bed and grabbed the remote control from the coffee table. By now every station would surely be reporting the news of the horrendous murder of Brooklyn Sims. *He would soon be famous!*

He took a final drag on his cigarette and crushed it out into an overfilled ashtray. He was excited and nervous at the same time and could feel his heart pounding against his chest as he switched on the television and began surfing through the channels. As he expected, every station was reporting the breaking news of the sensational murder at the Sims estate. The Artist settled on Fox News, where a soaking-wet reporter was standing at the foot of Brooke's long driveway. She was wearing a translucent rain poncho that failed to protect her from the wind and rain that was falling heavily from the sky.

The Artist gazed out the small window and saw the rain teeming down against the glass. The wind gusted and he could hear the huge leaves on the nearby palm trees smacking against one another. The rain blew sideways through a large crack in the window and was now puddling on his carpet. The Artist frowned and raised the volume on the television.

"This is Dede Erickson reporting to you live from the exclusive Laurel Canyons section of Hollywood Hills, where, last night tragedy struck with the brutal slaying of a young woman in the home of Hollywood superstar, Brooklyn Sims."

The camera zoomed in on the house and a small photograph of Skyler flashed on the bottom of the screen. The Artist jumped to his feet. He couldn't believe what he was seeing.

"The victim, Skyler Dawn, was said to be a close personal friend of Ms. Sims although there is no word as of yet from Ms. Sims and her spokesperson has declined to comment."

The Artist was furious. "No, no, no. How the fuck could this have happened!" he screamed. "It was Brooke in that pool. Red hair, her smell, had to be . . . her face." Then he thought for a moment. *Had he actually seen her face?* "It was her!" he roared, punctuating his last statement by lifting the coffee table and hurling it towards the window. It crashed through the glass and flew over the concrete walkway and railing, falling three stories into the half-filled swimming pool below.

"Fuck, fuck, fuck, her face!" he yelled, as he ran his hands through his hair and frantically paced back and forth in the small room. His mind raced a million miles an hour and his heart felt like it would beat out of his chest. He reached for the television and was about to send it over the railing when he saw a picture of Jake flash across the screen. Suddenly, he stopped, took a deep breath, and placed the television back down on its stand.

"FBI Deputy Director, Jake Chase, who flew into LAX late last night, has taken a curious interest in the homicide, but has refused comment. Some of you may remember Chase as the unassuming hero who single-handedly solved the Paramount bombing case, immediately propelling himself into the limelight. Well Jake, if you're listening, we need your help again. This is Dede Erickson, Fox News."

The Artist closed his eyes and began to rub his temples with the tips of his fingers. He needed to think. He had to regroup. *This was merely a setback, nothing to be concerned about.* On the bright side, now he wouldn't have to travel across the country. Jake Chase had come to him.

Slowly, he opened his eyes and gazed in the direction of the gaping hole where the window once was. The rain and wind had picked up and the small puddle on his carpet was quickly turning into a pond. He laughed in frustration and made his way back into the small kitchenette. He pulled open a drawer and retrieved a small bottle of pills. He twisted off the cap and poured in a mouthful. As he chewed them down, he reached for his BlackBerry and opened the file marked Pride. He toggled to Brooke's folder and begrudgingly moved her to the end of the queue. "Okay, Brooke, you get to breathe for a few more days," he said with a sneer. "It's time to step it up a bit. No more mistakes!" He knew that *she* was going to be completely furious with him, but what difference did the order make, as long as he got the job done.

CHAPTER 11

IT WAS ALMOST 7:00 AM BY THE TIME JAKE finally checked into his room at the Beverly Hills Hotel. He was completely wired and his brain was racing out of control, searching for answers. No matter how hard he tried, he just couldn't figure out the connection. The killer had somehow obtained his private e-mail account and sent him a warning. *No easy task*. It was the equivalent of finding out the President's e-mail address and sending him a complaint about your federal income taxes. *It was impossible.* He wondered if somehow the link could possibly be Paramount; either way the killer wanted his attention and he had certainly gotten it.

With sleep completely out of the question, Jake quickly changed into a pair of sweats and running sneakers and made his way down to the hotel gym. He glanced at his watch. It was 7:15 and, on a Saturday morning in LA, Jake had the place all to himself. He had just enough time to get in a good cardio workout, shower up and sit with Krycerick for an 8:30 breakfast meeting in the hotel restaurant. He climbed onto the treadmill and put his PDA into a small plastic cup holder. He then placed a finger on a tiny icon resembling a small mountain and the rubber platform began to move, slowly at first, but gradually Jake increased the pace to a fast sprint. His heart was racing, and he could feel the blood surging through his body. It was exhilarating. "Nothing better to clear the mind," he huffed. "Even if I haven't slept in 48 hours straight," he mumbled, shaking his head as he gazed around the empty room filled with idle exercise equipment.

Just then, his PDA began to rattle in the plastic cup holder. Keeping his pace, Jake reached over and pushed a button on the BlackBerry activating the hands-free speaker phone. "Jake Chase" he huffed, as he picked up speed on the treadmill.

"Jake, it's Jarvis. Who the heck is chasing you now?" Then he laughed nervously. "Just kidding. I figured you'd be working out."

Jake silently continued to run. He increased the treadmill's elevation. His hair was drenched with sweat and he was breathing hard through his mouth and nose.

Jarvis cleared his throat. "Look, Jake, I got a match on those prints you sent me from the phone at Brooklyn Sims' house." He paused for a moment. "Good movie . . . Anyway, they belong to a guy named Desi DiSisto. He's got a rap sheet as long as my left arm, including a double homicide that some lawyer got him off of on a technicality." Jarvis continued to read the rap sheet. "Huh, looks like both victims were family members. Killed them over drug money. Nice family!"

Jake continued to run, but switched off the speaker and brought the phone to his ear. "Listen, Jarvis, e-mail me everything you have on this DiSisto guy and while you're at it, send some men to pick him up." Jake looked back down at his watch. "I can be at the Sims' house by 9. Have him brought there."

"You got it, boss!"

Jake placed the PDA back down into the cup holder. He was now running at full speed up the side of a virtual mountain. His T-shirt was soaked and he could feel his lungs expand and contract as he pushed himself even harder. *It felt wonderful.*

Once again, his PDA began to vibrate. He glanced down at the caller ID and could see the caller was Diane. A smile came to his face as he pressed an icon and the treadmill slowly came to a halt. He stepped off the rubber platform, threw a towel over his head and brought the phone to his ear. "I was just thinking about you," he said.

He could hear laughter. "Sure you were," she said sarcastically. "Let me guess. You haven't slept all night and you're on the treadmill in the hotel gym running full blast, trying to figure out your next move."

Jake grinned as he dried his face and hair with the towel. "Hey, what are you doing up so early on a Saturday morning?"

Diane sighed. "I can't sleep. I have horrible heartburn from these two bowling balls inside me, and you know how much I hate being here alone."

Jake rested the towel around the back of his neck. "Tell ya what, Di Di; I think I'm going to be here a little longer than expected. Why don't you fly out and spend some time at the Malibu house? At least we'll be close.

"Diane paused, considering. "Okay, well, I have a little work to finish up at Blythedale Children's Hospital, but I can probably be out there by Monday, Tuesday latest."

Suddenly, Jake's phone began vibrate. He looked down at the caller ID. It was Krycerick. "I'm going to have to take this," he said, and then braced himself.

Diane let out a huff. "Fine. I'll phone you tonight when I know my schedule." Then she paused. "And Jake . . . please be careful!"

"Always!"

Jake transferred to the incoming call. He took a moment, closed his eyes, and switched gears. "What can I do for you, detective?" he asked, as he exited the gym in the direction of his hotel room. Whether he liked it or not, his workout was now officially over.

Krycerick's voice was emphatic. "Jake, you need to get to Brooklyn Sims place ASAP." He was out of breath and his voice was raspier than usual.

Jake stopped walking and let out a sigh. "What now?"

"Just get here as soon as you can . . . We found something."

By 8:30 a.m., Jake was once again pulling up the long driveway leading to Brooke's home. It had stopped raining and the sun shone in the sky. He pulled in behind one of the many news vans that were still camped out in front of the house. The media personnel were now properly contained behind yellow police tape by two uniformed officers from the LAPD, but they were still present in full force. One of the policemen gave Jake a nod as he quickly made his way to the front door and entered the home. To his surprise, it was extremely quiet, peaceful even. It was as if all of the hysteria from the previous night's events had somehow dissipated along with the wind and rain and was now replaced with the tranquil sunshine. *It was calm, Zen calm.*

Suddenly, the door to the patio slid open and Chief Krycerick came barreling into the living room. "Jake, you've gotta see this," he said, holding up an LAPD evidence bag containing the Oscar replica that The Artist had left under the bushes.

Jake was amazed at how those five words could somehow overpower the Zen-like tranquility and suddenly fill the room with stress. He took the bag from Krycerick and looked down at its contents. "An Academy Award?"

Krycerick grinned as he slipped on a pair of latex gloves. He took the evidence bag back from Jake, reached in and pulled out the small trophy. "We found this in the bushes next to the pool," he said. "It's a replica; you can get one in just about any store out here."

Jake grew impatient. "So, unless it has the killer's prints, which I'm pretty sure . . ."

Krycerick raised an oversized index finger in Jake's direction, slowly shaking it side to side. "Get a load of this, deputy director," he said, as he turned the golden statue around so that Jake could read the inscription.

Jake's eyes widened as he read the words "Shapiro Talent Agency." Suddenly, he understood why the killer had contacted him. This was the connection he was searching for. Without hesitation, he reached for his PDA and hit the speed dial button for Michael Jarvis' direct line.

Within seconds Jarvis answered. "What's up, Jake?"

"I need you to get me everything you can on the Shapiro Talent Agency, and I needed it two hours ago!"

Jarvis hesitated. "Lefty Shapiro? Wasn't he that guy who . . . ?"

"Jarvis!" Jake said excitedly. Then he paused. "I needed it two hours ago."

"I'm on it, Jake."

Jake put the phone back into his blazer pocket and ran his fingers through his hair. "What are you up to?" he muttered to himself, squinting his eyes in concentration.

Marty "Lefty" Shapiro had begun phoning Jake's office relentlessly immediately after the Paramount case. Although Jake had never actually spoken to him directly, his assistant Claudia had been fielding persistent phone calls from Lefty Shapiro promising to make Jake a huge Hollywood star with his mega-million-dollar story. Although Claudia would always politely decline, the calls didn't stop until Jake sent a couple of field agents to have a word with old Lefty. He hadn't heard from the Shapiro Agency since.

Krycerick turned his palms upward. He looked confused. "What?"

Jake took a deep breath and shook his head. "Let's just say I'm starting to understand how I'm tied into this whole mess."

There was a knock at the door.

Jake frowned. "I swear to God if that's a paparazzo, I'm gonna take his zoom lens and shove it up his . . ."

"Whoa," interrupted Krycerick. Then he laughed. "I'll get it," he said, as he made his way to the entrance and opened the front door.

Standing outside were three men, one of whom had his hands cuffed behind his back and was much smaller than the other two, who were both displaying FBI credentials. "May we come in?"

Krycerick looked over his shoulder in Jake's direction. "Honey, I think it's for you." He then stepped to the side, clearing a path. "Why not?" he said sarcastically, swinging his arm in a sweeping motion toward Jake. "Right this way."

One of the agents gave the handcuffed man a hard shove as the three walked past the Chief in Jake's direction. As big as the two FBI guys were, Krycerick still towered over both of them.

"Deputy Director, my name is Agent Billy Citarella and this is Agent Anthony Loman."

Loman gave a silent nod.

Citarella walked up to Jake and handed over a set of keys. "For the cuffs," he said.

"Hey, man, I know my rights," demanded DiSisto. "I want to speak to my attorney."

"Shut the fuck up, dickhead!" barked Loman as he shoved the handcuffed man over the side of the couch, causing him to fall face first into the cushions.

Citarella gave Jake a wink. "Let us know if we can be of any further assistance, Deputy Director."

The two men made their way back to the door, but before they exited, Loman turned to face Jake. "By the way, nice work on Paramount, Deputy Director."

Jake smiled. He then reached over and pulled DiSisto's face out of the cushions and helped him to an upright position. He took a seat across from him on a large wooden table situated directly in front of the couch. "Look, Desi, we just want to ask you a few questions."

"Fuck you! I know my rights. I got me the best lawyer in this city and I'm gonna sue the shit out of you and the whole . . ."

Suddenly, Krycerick smacked DiSisto in the back of the head so hard he lurched forward and fell head first into Jake. Jake grabbed the man by the face and threw him back into the couch.

DiSisto appeared stunned. "What the fuck was that for?" he asked nervously, looking back and forth between the two men.

Krycerick leaned in close over DiSisto's shoulder and brought his mouth close to his ear. "It's cause I can't stand fucking drug dealers," he replied angrily through clenched teeth.

Jake repositioned himself on the wooden table and smiled. "And I don't like fucking lawyers, Desi. So that's strike two."

DiSisto cowered. "Look fellas, I ain't had nothing to do with that chick gettin' killed."

Krycerick was still positioned behind the couch, still leaning in close. "Now, what chick might that be, Dizzy?"

Desi tried to slide himself away from Krycerick, but with his hands cuffed behind his back, wasn't having much success. He cleared his throat nervously. "You know, that hooker that got capped last night."

Once again, Krycerick smashed Desi in the back of the head, this time so hard that he fell to the floor. "Hey, have some fucking respect for the dead, shitbag."

Jake shook his head as he lifted Desi from the floor. He leaned in close and spoke slowly. "Listen, Desi, we know you were here last night. We got your prints off the phone," he said, nodding in the direction of the kitchen.

Desi shook his head from side to side, his smarmy expression long gone. "No, no, you guys got it all wrong. I was here last week, not last night. I used the phone to call my mother." He then looked back at Krycerick and prepared himself for another blow to the head. But surprisingly, none came. Instead, Krycerick stood up straight and shrugged his shoulders in Jake's direction.

Jake sighed, and then leaned in even closer. He breathed in through his nose several times, making a pronounced sniffing sound each time.

Krycerick gave him a curious stare.

Jake leaned back on the table. "Okay, you're right. Those prints might be from last week when you called . . ." he hesitated purposefully.

"My mother," interrupted Desi, nodding his head frantically.

"Right," continued Jake. "Your mother," he repeated, glancing over at Krycerick. Then he paused. "But let me ask you a question, Desi. How long do you think that cheap-ass Paco Rabanne cologne you're wearing would linger on the receiver?"

Krycerick smiled.

Desi leaned toward Jake. His voice was shaky. "Okay, okay, I was here last night, but I swear that chick was already capped . . . ." He froze momentarily and looked up at Krycerick apologetically. He took a breath and continued. "I mean, the young lady was already deceased when I arrived." He paused and looked between Jake and Krycerick, who were now both very interested in what Desi had to say. "She e-mailed me to bring party favors . . . an eight ball . . . that's all. I showed up with the coke, saw her dead in the hot tub." He looked at the ground, shaking his head side to side. "I freaked out, called the cops and split. I swear to God."

Jake gave Krycerick a nod. Krycerick then reached for a small walkie-talkie clipped to his belt and radioed one of the patrolmen who was stationed outside the house. "Marco, you wanna come in here and take this piece of shit to central booking?"

"Roger that, chief," crackled a voice through the radio.

Desi's eyes widened. "Wait . . . what for? I didn't kill her, I swear."

Krycerick leaned in close again. "Yeah, but you did admit to dealing drugs," he replied. Then he paused. "And you remember how I feel about drug dealers, dontcha, Dizzy?"

Jake stood from the table and shot Desi a cocky grin. "He doesn't like them very much."

CHAPTER 12

JAKE SWUNG OPEN THE GLASS doors and proceeded in the direction of the receptionist at The Shapiro Talent Agency. He glanced down at his watch: *11:30 a.m.* He knew time was running out and anticipated a second e-mail from the killer. He had sensed that the killings wouldn't stop with Skyler, and now with the clue the killer had left behind, he was sure of it. *Fucking psychos.*

Tyler stood from her desk and smiled warmly. Her hair was up in a bun held in place by two pencils bearing the Shapiro logo. She was dressed casually in a cotton knit sweater and tan slacks, her second outfit of the day. Her first had been ruined when she had accidently caused a cappuccino explosion in the kitchenette earlier that morning. "Good morning, welcome to the Shapir . . ." Suddenly, her eyes widened. She tilted her head sideways and pointed a finger. "You're Jake Chase," she said and actually appeared star-struck.

Jake nodded. "I'm here to see Marty Shapiro. I don't have an appointment."

Slowly, Tyler sank back into her seat and reached for the phone. "Mr. Chase, you're kind of a legend around here. I'm pretty sure he'll interrupt whatever he's doing to see you," she said, and then pressed Lefty's extension.

Suddenly, Jake could hear screaming coming through the receiver. "I said no interruptions!"

Tyler looked up at Jake and gave a shy smile, then covered her mouth with the palm of her hand. "But Mr. Shapiro, I have a Mr. Jake Chase here to see you," she whispered deliberately. There was a brief pause. Tyler nodded her head. "Yes, that Jake Chase." She hung up the phone and smiled. "He'll be just a minute."

Jake shook his head as he glanced down at his watch: 11:35.

Tyler looked over her shoulder in the direction of Lefty's office. She then leaned in on her desk resting on her elbows. She appeared a bit nervous and her voice was much lower now. "Um, Mr. Chase." She paused as she looked back a second time to make sure Lefty's door was still closed. "I never do this, and I could probably get fired for even asking, but I was wondering if you would mind very much giving me an autograph?" Just then she noticed her reflection in her computer monitor. Mortified, she pulled the two pencils from her bun allowing her hair to fall to her shoulders.

Jake forced a smile. "Look, I really don't think . . ."

"Well, well, well, Deputy Director Jake Chase," interrupted Lefty. "To what do we owe the privilege?" he cackled.

Jake glanced up at Lefty and a look of amazement came over his face. Tyler picked up on it and caught a slight chuckle in the palm of her hand. She smiled faintly and then began to shuffle through some papers on her desk, pretending to be busy.

Jake had assumed Marty Shapiro would have been a bit more polished, with better posture, and certainly thinner . . . a lot thinner. For sure, the small, squatty, bald man standing in the doorway wasn't the portrait of the Hollywood power player that Jake had imagined.

Lefty grinned. "So, Jake, I see you finally came to your senses and decided to let me represent you." He then looked down at Tyler and gestured in Jake's direction with his thumb. "The unassuming hero of the Paramount bombing case." He paused and shook his head. "The rights to that story alone are probably worth a hundred mil."

Jake frowned. "Listen, Mr. Shapiro, I'm here because I think your life may be in danger."

Tyler gasped as she brought her hand to her mouth. "Does this have something to do with that poor girl who was killed last night?"

Jake nodded then turned to face Lefty, gesturing in the direction of the door. "Look, is there someplace we can speak in private? Your office perhaps."

Lefty's grin widened. "Sure, kid, right this way," he replied as he stepped back, clearing a path for Jake to pass. Once Jake was inside, Lefty leaned his head out and whispered to Tyler. "Prepare three sets of our standard agency agreement." He then closed the door and followed Jake across the huge room. "Have a seat, kid," said Lefty," motioning to one of the guest chairs. He then fell back into his leather seat and leaned in over his desk. Then he smiled. "Six months I been leaving messages for you and it takes some slut hooker to get her head chopped off to get you into my office."

Jake remained standing. He reached into his blazer pocket, pulled out the Oscar that Krycerick had given him and set it down on the desk in front of Lefty.

Lefty eyed the small trophy, then looked up at Jake and smiled. "Cute, kid." He leaned back in his chair and put his feet on top of his desk, inches from the golden statue. "Sign up with my agency and I'll get you a real one of those by this time next year."

Jake shook his head in disbelief. *I can't believe how much I hate this fucking town.* Then he forced a smile. "Mr. Shapiro, I don't think you understand . . ."

"Kid, please . . . call me Lefty."

Jake's face tightened as if he had just bitten into a lemon. "I'd rather not," he said, shaking his head. He couldn't help think how much Marty Shapiro looked like he had just stepped off the pages of a comic book. Calling him Lefty would have been the icing on the cake.

Lefty frowned as he placed his feet back on the floor and leaned into his desk. He stared down at the Oscar momentarily then looked up at Jake. "Skyler Dawn was bad news." He paused and shook his head as a serious expression came upon him. "I warned Brooke to stay away from her, but she didn't listen."

Jake picked up the statue. His voice was more deliberate now. "This was a message from the killer, but I don't think Skyler Dawn was whom he was after." His eyes narrowed. "I think she just got in the way." Jake placed the Oscar back into his blazer pocket and continued. "I'm pretty sure whoever did this was there to kill Brooklyn Sims, and I have a strange feeling you're next."

For a moment Marty Shapiro appeared concerned. Then he began to laugh. "Come on, kid, this is LA. There's a dead hooker found in a hot tub every other day."

"All the same, is there anyone you can think of who would want to harm you or Ms. Sims?"

Lefty shook his head. "Brooklyn Sims was the exception to the rule." He paused considering. "Yeah, everyone in town liked her and that's rare in Hollywood." Suddenly, a wide grin stretched across his face. "Me, however, that's another story. I can think of at least a hundred people that wouldn't mind seeing my head hacked off in a swimming pool." Then he started to laugh.

Jake closed his eyes and pinched the bridge of his nose between his thumb and index finger. His head was starting to pound and he was growing impatient. He opened his eyes, pulled a business card from his blazer pocket and handed it over to Lefty. "My cell number is on the back." He turned and walked across the huge room to the door. "I'm staying at the Beverly Hills Hotel," he said, without bothering to turn around.

Lefty looked down at the card and frowned. Quickly, he jumped to his feet and hurried after Jake. "The Beverly Hills Hotel? Come on, kid, are you serious?" He sounded out of breath. "That place hasn't been . . ."

Suddenly, Jake stopped and turned to face Lefty. The abrupt move startled Lefty, and he skidded to a stop inches from Jake, nearly knocking into him. He took a step back and laughed nervously. "Look, kid, all I'm saying is you and I could do big . . . ."

"Hey!" interrupted Jake, pointing an angry finger in Lefty's direction. "How many times do I have to tell you? I've got no interest in you, this talent agency or the whole goddamn city for that matter!" Then he turned and reached for the door.

Lefty turned up the palms of his hands. "But, kid, I got Hefner's jet for the weekend. I'm thinking you and I can head down to Cabo with a few bunnies and work out a deal."

Jake turned to face Lefty one final time. "And another thing," he paused. "It's Deputy Director . . . Lefty." He pulled his blazer to the side exposing his Glock 9mm strapped into its leather shoulder harness. Then he smiled. "Call me kid again, and I'm gonna shoot you in the leg." Jake then turned and made his way for the exit, leaving a dejected Lefty Shapiro alone in his huge office. As he approached Tyler's desk he noticed something different about her. During his brief visit with Lefty, she had gone through some sort of transformation. With a fresh coat of makeup and her hair brushed back off her face, she looked more like a fashion model than a receptionist. Jake stopped in front of her desk and faced her. "Before I met with . . . ." he paused and squinted, considering. "Caron's Poivre?"

Tyler smiled. "Yes, actually it is," she said, as she sat upright in her seat. "Thank you for noticing, Mr. Chase."

Jake nodded. "My wife wears the same perfume."

Tyler deflated.

"Anyway . . . earlier, you asked me for my autograph."

Tyler smiled shyly. "Yes, if you wouldn't mind. You know, I never . . ."

But before she could finish, Jake tossed his card down onto Tyler's desk. "I'm staying at the Beverly Hills Hotel. My cell is on the back." He turned and began walking toward the glass doors. "I think someone is out to kill your boss. Call me when he does."

CHAPTER 13

IT WAS NEARLY 1:00 PM AND JESSE JAMES was making his way through the dimly lit lobby of The Palms Hotel and Casino just off the strip in downtown Las Vegas. As he crossed the hardwood floor and entered the casino, he could hear the high-pitched squeals echoing from the long rows of slot machines and the celebratory cheers coming from the over-crowded craps tables that lined the entranceway. The entire place was rockin'. However, the ambient noises of the casino appeared muffled by the loud music that was pumped through the multitude of speakers, strategically placed throughout the hotel. And it wasn't just any music that was being piped into the hotel lobby, elevators, corridors, restaurants and guest rooms. It was *Back Against the Wall*, the title track from Jesse's new album that was filling the air, and it made him smile.

As always, his entourage of usual suspects surrounded Jesse. Four men in all, Jessie's posse was composed of his two brothers, Luke and Robbie, who had recently been promoted to management positions within the James Organization, Joey-G, his chauffeur/bodyguard, and, Jesse's best friend, Nicky, who was in charge of making sure there was always plenty of Jesse's two favorite things: hookers and whiskey.

Jesse could feel commotion building around him as the group traversed the crowded casino, past the front desk in the direction of the VIP check-in lounge. He could hear the murmurings from every side and he loved it. *Is that him? That's Jesse James. Oh my God, I think I just saw Jesse James!*

It was a beautiful Saturday afternoon and the weather was above average for late October in Vegas, 85 degrees and sunny. The Palms was filled to capacity for the weekend with young, tanned, good-looking partygoers—perfect for Jesse and his posse. But the electricity he was causing was no different than in any hotel in any city, and, at 22, Jesse James' music career was through the roof and heading for the stratosphere.

Jesse and company were in town for a two-day long photo shoot for the cover of *GQ*. The group was being featured in a lengthy article appropriately titled *The New Look of Rock & Roll*. Why not? All five men were tall, dark and handsome with lots of body ink and multiple piercings. They all dressed in long, black leather overcoats, dark Armani button-down shirts and torn jeans. Each one resembled a rock star in his own right, but Jesse was the one with all the talent. He not only looked the part but also had the voice to back it up. He was the real McCoy and with a sold-out worldwide tour and his latest album going double platinum, he was unstoppable.

Jesse was just about to push open the door and enter the VIP lounge when suddenly he heard screams coming from the crowded casino behind him. Quickly, he turned and scanned the room, but could not detect where the noise was coming from. Just then, he noticed a young girl pushing her way through the crowd and calling out his name. Jessie squinted his eyes, trying to focus on the woman through the dark room. She had tanned skin that accentuated her bleached blond hair and was wearing only a small pink bikini. By the time Jesse realized what was happening, the woman had ripped off her top and was diving into his arms.

Instinctively, Jesse caught the half naked girl who promptly wrapped her arms and legs around him and shoved her tongue into his mouth as her girlfriends all snapped photos with their camera phones. Jesse could taste a mix of rum and suntan lotion on the young girl's lips as he carefully reached under her arms and peeled her off. Suddenly, the entire casino began to cheer and snap photos.

Jesse shook his head and smiled. "That'll do, sweetheart," he said to the topless woman, as he handed her over to Joey-G with her bare feet dangling in the air.

"I love you, Jesse," yelled the woman, with her arms flailing about in his direction, as Joey-G carried her back to her bikini-clad friends, who were all giggling and flashing away on their phone cameras.

Jesse laughed. "Yeah, I love you too, Princess."

The comment caused more applause and more jeers from the crowd, who all began chanting his name.

Jesse looked over at his two brothers, who were now both cracking up hysterically. He raised his palms to the ceiling and smiled. "What, like that never happens to you guys?" He then put his arms over their shoulders as they all made their way past two hotel security guards and crashed through the doors into the VIP lounge.

The Palms Hotel had designed the check-in lounge for superstars like Jesse, only A listers. In other words, you had to be the real deal to get in. The running joke among the hotel staff was that the lounge was Paris Hilton proof; even most of the high rollers the hotel would fly in on the private jet, who would drop millions at a single blackjack table, didn't qualify for admission. It was, in a word, private, and, in Vegas, private was important.

Although, the lounge was not only a convenient and discrete way for guests like Jesse to check into the hotel, it resembled a night club with its dark Italian marble floors, fully stocked bar and scantily clad cocktail waitresses. Once safely inside, the five men all fell into an assortment of leather chairs and sofas and began laughing. Jesse leaned forward on the sofa and pointed a finger at Nicky. "Look, man, I'm gonna need you . . ."

Nicky smiled and raised the palms of his hands to Jessie. "Already taken care of, Jess. The bikini chick's name is Kimbra Reese. She and her friends are in town for a bachelorette. They'll be at our suite tonight at 11."

Jesse grinned as he relaxed back into the sofa while the rest of the group high-fived Nicky, yelling and cackling in appreciation.

"Hello, gentlemen. My name is Nina. May I serve anyone?" asked a beautiful Asian cocktail waitress wearing a tight-fitting black dress and not much else. Then she smiled seductively at Jesse. "The usual, Mr. James?"

Suddenly, the raucous, testosterone-fueled banter of the men faded to silence.

Jesse nodded and two more cocktail waitresses appeared similarly dressed, equally as beautiful as the first. One was carrying a bottle of Jack Daniels, and the other a tray with eight glasses. "Mind if we join you guys?"

Jesse smiled. "Absolutely," he replied, as Robbie and Luke slid over and cleared room for the girls on the couch. Nina took a seat on Jesse's lap as the other two women poured out shots of whiskey. Nicky reached for one of the glasses and stood. He raised his glass and looked down at Jessie. Following his lead, everyone else raised his glass in unison. "To our good friend, Jessie," said Nicky, then he smiled. "Without you, the only way we'd ever see a place like this would be if we got a job here bartending." Then his smile turned into a grin. "And to think, we all gave you shit for joining the chorus in high school."

Suddenly, everyone began cheering as Jesse knocked back the whiskey in a single gulp. Joey-G let out a loud whistle and the whole group resumed their raucous laughter. One of the cocktail waitresses stood up and began refilling everyone's glass, starting with Jesse's.

"Excuse me, Mr. James, I don't mean to interrupt, but your sky villa is ready," shouted a young bellboy over the noisy group. Nervously, he handed over a leather satchel bearing the Palms emblem on its front.

Jesse took the satchel from the kid, looked inside the bag and shook his head in amazement. It contained ten magnetic keys to the villa, a bottle of Cristal champagne, several hundred dollars in chips and five vouchers for a hot stone massage at the hotel spa. He leaned in close to Robbie and Luke and chuckled. "I guess for 40 thousand dollars a night they don't have some obnoxious clerk toss your room key over the counter at you."

Luke shook his head in agreement. "Indeed they don't, bro. They hand it over to you in an expensive leather bag while gorgeous half-naked women sit on your lap and bring you booze."

"Um, I hate to bring this up," interrupted the bellboy, who appeared even more nervous than before. "And please understand that if I owned this place it would be no problem," he continued, as he nervously shifted his weight between feet.

For the second time the room fell silent as everyone's attention was now focused on the kid.

Jesse shot back his refill of whiskey. "What's your name, my man?"

Still rocking back and forth, the bellboy said, "Bob, Bob Triscari. But my friends call me Tris."

Jesse smiled. "You know, Tris, in Vegas they call that a tell," he said, pointing to the bellboy's feet.

The comment made Nina chuckle slightly.

Tris took a deep breath. "Okay, here's the thing, Mr. James. They told me that the last time you stayed here at The Palms you caused over 60 thousand dollars worth of damage to one of their rooms." He then handed over an envelope. "Here's' the list."

Jesse grinned. "No leather satchel for this one, huh, Tris?"

Again Nina chuckled, and this time the other two women joined in.

Jesse opened the envelope and pulled out an itemized bill. He leaned over to the woman sitting on the couch next to him. "Be a doll and pour us another round. And, love, fetch an extra glass for Tris, would ya."

"Right away, Mr. James."

Jesse looked down at the bill and began nodding his head as he read through the long list. Suddenly, his eyes narrowed. He angled the letter toward his brothers and pointed to number twenty-seven on the list.

"The Picasso," said Robbie and Luke in unison.

Jesse started laughing. "Oh yeah, I forgot about that." He then looked back down at the page and continued reading. "Yup, it seems right," he said, nodding his head in agreement. He then handed the bill to Luke. "Take care of this, will ya bro."

"You got it, Jess," said Luke, as he stood from his seat and handed the envelope back to Tris along with an American Express Black Card.

Tris appeared to be relieved. "Thank you, Mr. James, it'll just be a few minutes. I just have to bring this to my boss," he said, as he quickly retreated for the door.

Jesse reached for his glass that was once again filled with Jack Daniels. He gave Robbie a nudge in the ribs with his elbow and winked at one of the cocktail waitresses. "Oh, hey, Tris, one more thing." He smiled. "You tell your boss to charge us double."

Tris turned to face the group. He appeared baffled. "You want me to do what?"

"You heard me. A hundred-twenty grand."

One of the waitresses let out a slight yelp and then quickly tried to take it back by covering her mouth with her hand.

"But why?" asked Tris hesitantly.

Jesse grinned. He then tilted his glass to each of his brothers, who both looked at him curiously. "Cause we're gonna trash another one!"

CHAPTER 14

WITH TEN SECONDS LEFT ON THE CLOCK Trevor Hash looked up at the scoreboard from the 50-yard line of the filled-to-capacity LA Memorial Coliseum. With 93 thousand screaming fans in attendance, it had been a grueling 55 minutes of hard-hitting, helmet-to-helmet, smash-mouth football, and with only seconds left on the game clock, Notre Dame led by a field goal. Trevor struggled to catch his breath as he brought a bloodied hand to the side of his helmet and undid the snap on his chin strap. He raised his helmet to his forehead and looked to the sidelines in the direction of the USC offensive coordinator, who was signaling for a short pass. With one time out left, all Trevor had to do was get the ball within 35 yards, call time, and leave it to special teams to tie the game and force overtime. Was that the smart play? Absolutely. Was that what Trevor was going to do? Hardly. Trevor gave one more look in the direction of the scoreboard, pulled down his helmet and called his team into the final huddle of the game. "All right," he commanded, "anyone here wanna blow our undefeated season to these Irish pussies?"

"No way," grunted a few of the offensive linemen.

Trevor spit out his mouthpiece. "I said does anyone here wanna blow our fucking undefeated season to these fucking Irish pussies!" he repeated, this time far more deliberately.

"No fucking way!" barked back every player in the huddle. *He had their full attention and he was in complete control.*

Trevor nodded confidently. "That's what I fucking thought," he yelled back, making eye contact with each man. He was completely pumped. His adrenaline level was off the charts and he knew exactly what he had to do to bring home another USC victory and save his Heisman from the auction block. "Now, is anyone here tired?"

"No, Trevor!"

"Anyone here fucking tired!"

"No fucking way, Trevor!"

Trevor looked up in the direction of USC's 290-pound All-American offensive lineman, Marc Sanzeri. There was a huge gash on the bridge of his nose and bloodstains on his jersey. "San, you fucking tired?"

"Just gettin' warmed up, Trev."

Marc Sanzeri wasn't your typical Pillsbury Doughboy lineman. He was solid muscle and that was exactly what Trevor needed to plow a path into the end zone.

Trevor nodded. "Good. Now here's the thing, boys," he said once again addressing the huddle. "I'm not too happy leaving our undefeated season in the hands of special teams." Trevor paused and looked around. He could see the unfettered determination in the eyes of every man. They were bloodied and they were exhausted but they were warriors, each and every one of them. He then reached over and put his hand on Sanzeri's shoulder. "San, I need you to clear a path for me. You do that and I promise you and every man standing here that I will bring this ball to the end zone and put another check in the win box for all of us.

"Consider it done!" grunted San.

"Okay, gentlemen, on three."

"One . . . two . . . three . . . break!"

As Trevor took his place behind the center he looked up into the stands. What he saw was a sea of colors that all seemed to blend together into a gigantic collage of screaming fans. The noise level in the Coliseum was off the charts. He had to scream at the top of his lungs just to be heard by his teammates. He gave one last look at the game clock, and then proceeded to call the final play of the game. "Blue forty-two . . . blue forty-two, strong side right . . . strong side right . . . hut . . . hut . . . hike."

Suddenly the ball was in his hands and he sprang into action. There was no thought involved, just pure reflex. The game of football came easily to him, and it had ever since he was 7. Trevor could hear the sound of mashing helmets as bodies clashed all around him. With Sanzeri directly in front of him plowing down opponents like a Mack truck running through a cornfield, Trevor made his way over the 50 yard line into Irish territory. The only sound he could hear now was the sound of his own heavy breathing. The loud noises of the bustling stadium and the crashing bodies all faded away. *He was in the zone.* Suddenly, two Notre Dame players appeared out of nowhere and simultaneously hit Sanzeri, one high and one low. San fought hard to stay on his feet but crashed to the ground with a thunderous boom. For a brief moment the ambient sounds of the stadium penetrated Trevor's consciousness, but as he gazed up at the scoreboard to see the time switch to zero seconds he kicked it into overdrive. He leaped over the two players

San had managed to take down with him and raced for the end zone.

Twenty . . . fifteen . . . ten . . . suddenly a Notre Dame defenseman appeared out of nowhere and was standing in between him and victory. Without wasting a second Trevor leapt into the air, tucked his shoulder under his flying body and somersaulted five feet above the lineman and into the end zone.

All at once, the already boisterous crowd stood to their feet and erupted into a pandemonium of cheers and celebration. The sound was so loud that it actually made the seats rattle. Trevor picked himself up off the ground and ripped out a clump of grass from his facemask. He flipped the ball to one of the officials, looked up at the scoreboard and smiled: USC 6, Notre Dame 3. He clapped his hands together hard. "Yeah," he grunted, as he undid his chin strap and sprinted in the direction of the USC tunnel. The entire stadium was going absolutely crazy cheering and chanting his name, paying little mind to the kicker as he split the uprights to score the point after. He could feel the blood pumping through his veins and the adrenaline rushing throughout his entire body as he joined the rest of his team in a celebration of high-fives as they all jogged into the tunnel toward the locker rooms. He could hear the sound of his pounding heart mixed with the clicking of cleats on the cement floor and echoing off the tunnel walls as the team charged through double steel doors and burst into the USC locker room like a herd of wild bulls.

"Fucking A!" shouted two linebackers as they head-butted one another and fell into a manly hug. "That's right, baby! Sugar Bowl, here we come!"

Trevor approached his locker and winced as he slowly sat down on the wooden bench. He looked around to make sure no one had noticed, but everyone was too busy celebrating. He took a deep breath and carefully raised his jersey revealing a huge bruise on his left rib cage. He clenched his teeth and gently brought his fingers to the tender area. Even the slight touch sent alarming sharp pains through his body. The adrenalin rush was wearing off and he was now finding that even breathing caused discomfort. Trevor shook his head and slowly began to lower his uniform when suddenly a huge hand smacked him in the back of the head forcing him to lurch forward and poke himself in the ribs.

"Awesome fucking run, Handsome," barked Sanzeri, whose mangled nose and bloodstained jersey made him look like more like a maniacal killer than a sophomore at USC. "You da man!"

Trevor bit his lip and gasped for air. "No . . . you da man," he mumbled, trying to conceal the pain in his voice. He exhaled slowly and forced a smile. "Great stick."

"Fucking A right," shouted San, as he ran off to join the other linemen who were looking for Coach Gilberti with a full jug of Gatorade.

With his hand held guardedly over his ribs, he slowly took off his uniform, wrapped a towel around his waist and made his way to the whirlpool. The celebration in the locker room was starting to subside, and as the rush of the day's victory began to fade, his head started to pound. He knew that the team's physician would probably be busy stitching up gashes and taping broken fingers, pretty common after a hard-hitting game like today's, but Trevor decided to try his office anyway.

"Yo, doc, you here?" he asked, as he inched open the door to the physician's office and peered in. He was still holding his ribs. The pressure seemed to make the throbbing subside.

"Hey, Trevor, great game," said Dr. Hickey with a warm, grandfatherly smile. "I was just about to head out to the locker room," he said, gesturing to his medical bag on the floor by the door. "You caught me in the nick of time." He then gave Trevor a curious look and paused. "What's wrong, son?"

Trevor wondered if it was the Doc's 40 years of medical training that gave him away or if he just looked that fucked up. "Caught a helmet in the side," he said, turning his body so that the bruised ribs faced the doctor.

Hickey looked unfazed. "I see," he said, as he walked over to Trevor. He knelt down beside him and gently ran his fingers along Trevor's ribs.

Trevor gasped.

Dr. Hickey stood. "I don't think they're broken." He then walked to his desk and reached into a drawer. He pulled what appeared to be a piece of cardboard about the size of a small paperback book with eight oval-shaped pills vacuum-sealed to its front. In red letters were the words, Oxycontin Sample Pack. He handed it to Trevor. "One every eight hours." He looked serious. "On a full stomach."

Trevor nodded. "Got it. Thanks, Doc." Then he turned to exit the room.

"And I want to see you in a few days to have another look at those ribs," called Hickey.

Trevor slowly lowered himself into the steaming hot whirlpool. Most of the other players had left except for a few who were lingering around giving interviews in the front of the locker room. He exhaled deeply as he let the bubbling water massage his aching muscles. The two Oxycontin he had taken were starting to kick in, and he was now feeling no pain. He glanced up at the clock on the wall. It was almost 7 p.m. and he was starved. He closed his eyes and rested his head on the ledge of the whirlpool. He felt himself going in and out of consciousness when he heard a sudden noise that jolted him back to reality. He looked up at the clock: 10 p.m. "Fuck," he shouted as he jumped to his feet. The abrupt movement caused severe pain in his ribs sending electric waves through his entire body. His legs buckled and he fell out of the whirlpool and onto the floor, face down. "Nice going, Trevor," he groaned, as he lay there naked in the dark room. He gave a slight chuckle, then lifted himself off the floor and reached for his towel. Suddenly, he heard the noise again. This time is was a lot louder and a lot closer. *He wasn't alone.* Someone was in the room with him. He squinted against the darkness and could see a figure walking towards him. "Hello," he said nervously. "Can I help you?"

He heard giggling. He was completely baffled as he squinted harder to see who was quickly approaching him. Then the object came into focus. It was Naomi Brown, the reporter from *Sporting News.*

"Hi there, Handsome."

Trevor was speechless.

Naomi grinned as she pressed her body tightly against Trevor's. "What? No quick come back? I'm so disappointed," she said, as she reached under Trevor's towel. "Oh my," she said. "This certainly isn't a disappointment, though."

Trevor was in shock. He stood there leaning against the whirlpool, his entire body seemed frozen in place as Naomi dropped to her knees and undid his towel, letting it fall to the floor.

She smiled seductively and looked up at Trevor. "Very, very nice, Handsome." She then reached into her purse with one hand while holding him with the other. "I have something here I think you are going to enjoy, Handsome." Instantly, her smile vanished and was replaced by an evil grin. She tightened her grip on Trevor causing him to gasp, but before he had a chance to react she pulled a pair of gardening shears from her purse, brought them to his manhood, and squeezed the handles tightly.

Trevor screamed in earth-shattering agony as he flailed about in the bubbling water, taking in a mouthful. Quickly, he leaned over the side and began coughing and gasping for air. "Fuck!' he screamed as he looked around the room trying to focus. It was completely empty. He looked at the clock on the wall: 7:12. "Holy shit!" he exclaimed, as he reached between his legs to make sure he was still all attached. "It was just a fucking dream." He grabbed the package of Oxycontin with its two missing pills. He put his hand on his forehead, shaking his head in amazement. "Note to self. Never exceed recommended dosage." He exhaled a sigh of relief and stepped out of the whirlpool. He was still a bit disoriented as he made his way to his locker. The entire place was deserted, and Trevor assumed that most of the team was well into a keg at one of the campus parties. He was still thinking about that horrible dream, so much so that he didn't notice the man standing behind him with the machete looming over his head, cocked and ready to barrel down upon him.

"Nice run, Handsome," whispered The Artist, so faintly that Trevor wasn't sure if he had imagined it. But when he turned around he was met with the long blade of the machete as it tore through his neck, severing his head from his body.

The Artist was emotionless. He took out a handkerchief and wiped the blood that had splattered onto his face and shirt. He was dressed in a USC custodian's uniform, name badge and all. He reached into his pants pocket and retrieved a BlackBerry he had borrowed earlier from some student's backpack, typed a message to Jake and hit the send button. He then threw the PDA against the wall, smashing it to pieces. The Artist didn't blink and was void of all expression as he placed the bloodied machete into his satchel and took out a small golden statue with the words Shapiro Talent Agency on its base. He carefully placed the award in front of Trevor's locker and exited the locker room undetected.

CHAPTER 15

IT WAS NEARLY 7:00 P.M. AND JAKE WAS growing impatient as he waited in Chief Krycerick's cramped office on the fourth floor of LA police headquarters. He glanced down at his watch for the umpteenth time and sighed. He had been sitting in the same spot for over a half hour, waiting for a status meeting.

Krycerick's office was antiquated and dusty with an old steel desk in the corner of the room. In front of it stood two imitation leather chairs, both bearing distinct worn spots in the seats from years of use. Beside the desk was a metal filing cabinet upon which sat a sad-looking potted plant that seemed to be on its last legs. At the base of the ceramic pot was a clump of dry soil that trailed curiously along the top of the cabinet and spilled down onto the floor below. The walls behind the desk were adorned with a multitude of plaques and framed letters of commendation for services to the police department above and beyond the call of duty. There was an assortment of crookedly hung pictures of a younger Krycerick standing with high-ranking members of the department and various city officials. There was even a framed photo of him receiving some sort of a medal from President Reagan. In the midst of the confusion, unframed and pinned to the wall with a thumb tack, was a diploma from Cornell School of Medicine. It's four corners were dog-eared and the document was yellowed with age. The array of accolades were impressive and at the same time incongruous with the space. Most interestingly, they came to a sudden halt in the late `80s. It was as though the young man in the photos, whose career appeared to be on the fast track to certain success, had mysteriously vanished. It struck Jake as odd and somewhat sad.

Just then the door to Krycerick's office swung open. It was his secretary, Kathy Murphy, and she was backing herself into the room after managing to open the door with her elbow. She was carrying a large stack of files that she steadied with the bottom of her chin. Immediately, Jake stood and hurried to help the struggling woman. "Here, let me give you a hand with that," he said, reaching out to take the files from her.

Kathy smiled. "It's okay. I got it, Deputy Director." She then dropped the stack onto the filing cabinet with a loud thud. The vibration caused the small plant to topple and spill out another clump of dirt onto the cabinet and floor. Kathy pursed her lips and blew the hair from her face as she uprighted the sickly plant. "He'll only be a few more minutes," she said, as she turned to face Jake. "He's questioning a perp on a triple homicide." She paused shaking her head. "Gangbangers."

Jake nodded and returned to his seat. He pointed to the wall behind Krycerick's desk. "Interesting career."

Kathy placed her hands on her hips and scanned the haggard wall of crooked frames and accolades. "Yes, it certainly was," she replied, as she walked up to the wall and straightened out a few of the more lopsided photos. "And I've been here for the whole wild ride."

Jake stayed silent.

"You know, he's really a great guy." She turned to face Jake. Her voice was more deliberate now. "He just caught some bad breaks."

Jake looked confused. "I don't understand."

Kathy gave a sad smile and then continued. "It was in the early `90s, just after the whole Rodney King mess." She paused and shook her head. "That was a really bad time for this city," she muttered to herself. "Nails," she paused. "I mean Eddie, had been out on a routine bust . . . drug dealers . . . real mean bunch . . . ranking members of the Crips." A longer pause. "Anyway, Eddie and his partner were cuffing these three guys when one of them reaches down and grabs Eddie's partner's gun and begins firing wildly." Kathy seemed to be growing uncomfortable, as if she had been through the story a million times and hated it more and more each time. "Eddie took a bullet in the shoulder. His partner wasn't as lucky," she said.

Jake shook his head as he looked up at the wall of old photos that spoke volumes of this man's life. He looked back at Kathy. "He seems to be doing okay now."

Kathy smiled. She glanced up at the wall and then looked back at Jake. "Yeah, well unfortunately, the story doesn't end there, Deputy Director." She walked to the front of the desk and leaned against it. "After the funeral, Eddie hit the bottle pretty hard. As quickly as his career took off . . ." She hesitated searching for words. "Well, let's just say it went just as quickly in the other direction. After about a year of that nonsense, his wife left him and took the two kids with her. Then Eddie just got downright mean, and after a shoving match with the wrong guy in the department, he was busted down to desk duty."

Jake cocked his head. "Yeah, but now . . . I mean . . . he's in charge of this unit," he said, with question in his voice.

Kathy's smile widened. "That just goes to show you, Deputy Director. Good things do happen to good people," she said, as she stood and walked behind the desk. She pulled open the bottom drawer, retrieved a folded newspaper clipping and grinned. "He doesn't know that I know he has this," she said, handing it over to Jake.

Jake took the news clipping from Kathy and looked down at the headline. TOUGH AS NAILS COP RESCUES 4 CHILDREN FROM BURNING BUILDING. It was dated June 16, 2002. The article detailed how Eddie had run into the inferno against the protests of the fire department, which had deemed the building too unstable and were pulling out. There was a photo of him charging out of the blaze while carrying four little kids—two under each arm.

"Pretty amazing, huh, Deputy Director?"

Jake handed the clipping back to Kathy and nodded. "Yeah. Pretty amazing, indeed."

Kathy replaced the clipping in the bottom drawer. "It was his redemption. Since that day he hasn't touched a drop of alcohol, got his career back on track, and even made peace with his ex." She chuckled. "Plus, came out of it with a pretty cool nickname, if I do say so."

Just then the door to the office swung open and a tired looking Eddie "Nails" Krycerick lumbered in. "Who has a cool nickname?" he asked.

Kathy gave Jake a wink and headed for the door. "I left you a little light reading, boss," she said, as she nodded at the stack of files.

Krycerick looked at the pile and frowned. "Thanks," he replied as he walked in Jake's direction.

Jake stood and extended his hand to Krycerick. "Listen, Chief, I haven't got much time, so why not fill me in on what you've found out?"

Krycerick nodded as he walked behind his desk and fell back into his chair. He glanced over at the stack of files and shook his head. "Yeah, I'm really sorry to keep you waiting, Jake. We had these three kids killed in a drug-related shootout." Suddenly his tired look was replaced with one of sadness. "Gangbangers." He then reached under his desk and opened the door to a compact refrigerator and took out a small cardboard container of chocolate milk. The word Quik was written on the front of the container along with the picture of a bunny wearing a necklace with the letter "Q" dangling around his neck. Krycerick held the container in Jake's direction. "Want one?"

Jake let out an impatient chuckle in amazement and raised the palms of his hands to Krycerick. "Chief, I'm a bit pressed for time here."

Krycerick placed the container of milk on his desk. "Of course," he said, as he brought the palm of his hand to the back of his neck. He looked disgruntled. "Unfortunately, we're no further along than we were this morning. According to Ms. Sims, nothing was missing from the home, so that pretty much rules out this being a botched robbery."

Jake rested his elbows on his knees and leaned forward. "DiSisto?"

"His story checked out. He's a drug dealer and a low life, but he's not our killer."

"What about the girl's body?"

Krycerick reached for a file on his desk and handed it to Jake. "Here is the report from the medical examiner's office. There were no signs of rape or any kind of struggle." He then folded back the cardboard flaps on the top of the container and took a huge swig of chocolate milk.

Jake opened the file and leafed through several gruesome photos of Skyler Dawn's headless body. There were also several of her in better days. She was actually a strikingly beautiful woman, with long strawberry-blond hair and deep blue eyes. Jake stared down at a shot of Skyler and Brooke sitting together at a nightclub and couldn't help notice how much the women looked alike. They could have been sisters. He began to read Dr. Bonina's report, but stopped when he got to the description of the slaying.

The killer used what appears to be an elongated knife (probably a sword or machete). Straight blade—no jags—2 or 3 feet in length. Critical lacerations beginning on back posterior along the cervical curve of the neck between the atlas vertebra and the axis vertebra (C1 and C2).

Krycerick raised an eyebrow. "You see something?"

Jake closed the file. "It's just a hunch," he said, sliding it across the desk to Krycerick.

Krycerick gulped down the last of the milk, crushed the container in his fist and tossed the remains into a pail by the door. "Yeah, well, if memory serves me, your hunches are usually spot on."

Jake stood to his feet and ran his fingers through his hair. He remained silent for a moment, concentrating. "You know, the medical examiner's report says that the victim was struck from the back at the base of her neck."

"Yeah," replied Krycerick. "Poor thing never saw it coming."

Jake nodded. "True, but it also means that the killer never saw whom he was approaching."

Krycerick tilted his head sideways. "What are you getting at?"

Jake reached for the file and flipped it open to the photo of the two women at the club. "Have you noticed how much Brooklyn Sims and Skyler Dawn look alike?" Jake asked, angling the file to Krycerick.

Krycerick stared down at the photo. "Yeah, now that you mention it."

"I think the killer went to the house that night looking for Brooke and got the wrong girl." He looked down at the file and pointed to the photo. "I mean, same build, same hair length, same hair color even."

Krycerick nodded. "Yeah, the killer would have no reason to believe that it wasn't Brooke in her own hot tub." Then he paused. "But why Brooklyn Sims? Everyone seemed to like her. Only got good press." He chuckled to himself. "Kinda rare these days."

Jake shrugged. "Not sure yet, but her agent is Lefty Shapiro. Somehow, I think he's got something to do with all this."

Krycerick let out a sarcastic laugh. "That fat fuck represents half of this town."

"Yeah, when I showed him the academy award with his name . . ."

Jake was suddenly interrupted by the sound of his BlackBerry. He reached to the inside pocket of his blazer and retrieved the phone. "Fuck!" he screamed, as he read the e-mail The Artist had sent. "So much for fair warning."

Krycerick stood and proceeded around to the front of the desk. "Is it from our man?"

Jake nodded and handed the BlackBerry to Krycerick. "If Trevor Hash is represented by Shapiro, my hunch just got a lot stronger."

Deputy Director,

I don't think Trevor Hash will be available for next week's game.

Can you guess who will be next?

The Artist

CHAPTER 16

THE ENTIRE USC CAMPUS WAS ON COMPLETE LOCKDOWN as Jake and Chief Krycerick crossed Menlo Avenue and made their way in the direction of the LA Coliseum. It was nearly 8:00 p.m. and the night air brought an unusual chill to the normally warm southern California sky. The earlier fanfare had long since dissipated, and the main entrance to the massive building was now blocked off by yellow police tape, with teams of patrolmen stationed at every other doorway. If the killer was somehow still in the Coliseum, he wasn't getting out.

Jake flashed his credentials to a series of stationed police personnel as he and Krycerick ducked under the yellow tape and made their way to the front doors. "It's like Paramount all over again," Jake yelled to Krycerick, over the loud buzzing from two LAPD choppers hovering overhead. He reached for the door, but took one last look behind him before he entered the building. The street was lined with cop cars, fire trucks and ambulances, and now the media was beginning to arrive in throngs. Word was out and the killer, whoever he was, certainly had everyone's full attention.

The two men made their way down a long tunnel toward the USC locker room, which was now the latest crime scene. There were uniformed personnel present in the large hallway but not nearly as many as outside the building. It was a pay grade thing. The closer you were allowed to the actual crime scene, the higher on the food chain you had to be.

"Hey Nails, right this way," came the voice of a young plain-clothes detective who was stationed outside a maroon-and-gold painted door with the words 'Authorized Personnel' stenciled across it.

"Thanks, Jimmy," replied Krycerick as the two men proceeded through the door.

Jake entered the USC Trojans locker room first, and it was like walking onto the set from a horror movie. It was surreal. He was in the locker room of the USC football team and lying in front of him was the lifeless body of a young man.

The ceiling above Trevor's body was drenched in his blood, so much so that droplets were forming and trickling down like raindrops onto one of the benches beside him, making a rhythmic, pattering sound. The effect was eerie. The lockers, mirrors and walls were splattered and a river of red had traveled down the hallway and formed a small pool under Dr. Hickey's door.

Jake felt a hand on his shoulder. It was Dr. Bonina. She had dark circles under her eyes and she looked exhausted.

"Hello, Deputy Director," she said, forcing a slight smile.

"Hello, Doctor," he replied, as he gazed around the large room. Beside himself and Chief Krycerick, there were only a few detectives and a handful of technicians from Bonina's office. He shook his head and slipped on a pair of latex gloves. "What have you got so far?"

Bonina frowned. "Besides the shattered remains of a PDA, unfortunately not much," she replied, nodding to what appeared to be hundreds of tiny pieces of plastic scattered around the floor beneath a long row of lockers. Each piece was meticulously tagged with a color-coded exhibit marker. "We're pretty sure the killer used it to contact you," she continued. "We'll know more in a few days." She then looked down at her notes and began to read. "The victim is Trevor Hash. He was found by one of the custodians about the same time you received the e-mail." She paused and nodded in the direction of Krycerick and two detectives, who were in the middle of taking a statement from a small, grey haired man wearing a custodian's uniform. "We calculate time of death to be at around 7:00 p.m. The cause of . . ." she hesitated and looked up from her notepad. "He didn't give you any warning this time, did he?"

Jake shook his head.

Bonina sighed and continued reading. "The cause of death, decapitation by a straight, un-serrated blade . . ."

"Two or three feet in length?" Jake interrupted. Then he looked in the direction of Trevor's body. The blood had stopped dripping from the ceiling and was now beginning to clot. "Same weapon used on Skyler Dawn?"

"Most likely," replied Bonina. "Probably a sword or machete of some sort. But this time the initial entry was from the front."

"I guess he wanted to make sure he got the right person this time," interrupted Jake.

Bonina closed her note pad. "Jake, what the heck is going on here? I have to tell you this is scaring the hell out of me."

Jake shook his head. "I'm not sure yet, Doctor. I have some theories but they're all pretty thin," he said, as he made his way to Trevor's body.

"How thin?" asked Bonina, following him across the room.

Jake found a blood-free spot on the carpet and knelt down beside the headless body. "Anorexic," he murmured, as he leaned forward and retrieved the small golden statue The Artist had left beside Trevor's locker. As he expected, the words Shapiro Talent Agency were written across its base. "Chief, you wanna come have a look at this," Jake said, returning to his feet.

Krycerick handed his card to the old man, gave one of the detectives a pat on the shoulder and made his way to Jake and Dr. Bonina. "Let me guess—The Shapiro Agency?"

"Yeah," replied Jake. "That fat fuck is beginning to get on my nerves." He handed the statue to Krycerick. "Have your lab dust this and then make sure it gets to Michael Jarvis at Quantico. I already sent him the one we found at Brooklyn Sims' house."

"You got it, Jake."

He then turned to face Bonina although he was really addressing them both. "Doctor, I'm going to need you to send a copy of your notes over to Chief Krycerick." He looked at the Chief. "Add them to Skyler Dawn's file and messenger everything to my attention at the Beverly Hills Hotel. I want it all by midnight."

Both Chief Krycerick and Dr. Bonina nodded in agreement.

Jake looked back down at the body. He cocked his head sideways. "What's this?" he mumbled to himself as he squinted at a blood-soaked object clenched in Trevor's fist. He knelt on the ground and leaned in close. "Dr. Bonina, have you a set of medical tweezers?"

"Of course, Jake," she replied, motioning to one of the technicians. "Christopher, please get the Deputy Director a set of medical tweezers."

Jake took one of the tweezers from the technician and carefully reached over the body. Gently, he placed the tip on the bloody object in Trevor's hand and slid it free. He stood to his feet, removed the object from the tweezers and studied it closely.

"What is it, Jake?" asked Krycerick curiously as everyone in the room looked on with hopeful anticipation.

Jake sighed and handed the object to Dr. Bonina. He could feel his pulse begin to rise as he clenched his teeth angrily. "It's nothing." He paused. "A red herring."

Bonina looked down at her hand. "Oxycontin?"

Jake walked into the center of the locker room. He was angry, tired and sick of the cat-and-mouse bullshit. "Okay, people, listen up!" All eyes were on Jake. "This guy's starting to get on my fucking nerves." He looked around to make sure he had everyone's undivided attention. *He did.* "Now, there are at least 80 players on this team, not to mention a head coach, a dozen assistant coaches, trainers, team directors, and . . ." he gestured to the package of Oxycontin Bonina was now tagging with a blue exhibit marker . . . "a goddamn team physician." He took a deep breath and exhaled slowly. "That's at least a hundred people in this locker room alone. Now someone had to see something!" He looked around the room and pointed to one of the detectives. "Son, what's your name?"

"Sagiv, sir, Detective First Grade Paul Sagiv."

"Okay, Detective First Grade Paul Sagiv. I want anyone and everyone who was in this locker room after today's game outside in that hallway in two hours." Jake looked down at his watch. "That's 11:00 p.m. sharp, got it?"

"Got it," replied Sagiv, and then darted for the exit.

Jake then turned to face Chief Krycerick and Dr. Bonina. "Okay guys, I'm gonna need forensics on both homicides in my hotel room by midnight."

Bonina nodded.

"And LAPD has 48 hours to process this evidence." Jake said, pointing to the array of exhibit markers. "Then I want everything re-bagged and messengered out to Quantico."

"You got it, Jake," replied Krycerick.

Just then Jake's BlackBerry began to vibrate. He held up his index finger to Krycerick and Bonina as he brought the phone to his ear. "Jake Chase."

"Hey, Jake, it's Jarvis."

Jake covered his phone with the palm of his hand and nodded at Krycerick and Bonina. "I have to take this," he said, and then proceeded to a quiet section of the locker room. "Okay Michael, give me some good news."

"Well boss, as usual, your hunch was correct. Trevor Hash is . . . um, I mean, was, represented by your old pal Lefty Shapiro."

Jake silently watched as Trevor's body was being fitted into a large black body bag. There was desolation throughout the room. Unlike the previous night, there was no chitter-chatter among the forensic team, no conversations among the detectives about sports trivia, and it struck Jake as odd that the death of one individual could cause such a different reaction in complete strangers than the death of another. Just because one happened to be able to throw a football.

"Here's the real kicker," Jarvis continued. "He just signed a multi-million dollar deal to play ball with the San Diego Chargers."

Jake shook his head. "I somehow doubt that has anything to do with it."

There was a brief silence. "Well, you know best," replied Jarvis, sounding a bit deflated. "Oh, I almost forgot. The e-mail—the one from last night—it came from a PDA belonging to a woman named Lisa Harris. She's a bartender at a trendy spot in downtown LA called the Bean Post. Said she had her purse stolen the day before and her BlackBerry was in it. We sent a couple of guys down there today, and her story checks out."

Jake closed his eyes and pinched the bridge of his nose. His head was starting to throb from lack of food and sleep. "And tonight's?"

"And tonight's" repeated Jarvis, "came from a USC student named Alisha Raeburn. We tracked her through the Verizon account to one of the campus apartments. We have a field agent on his way there now, but don't get your hopes up. I kinda doubt that Alisha's the killer."

"Yeah, I'm sure it's the same story as the bartender," replied Jake. He paused and thought for a moment. "Okay, Michael, good work." He was about to hang up. "Oh, hey Mike, you still there?"

"Yeah, boss?"

"We're messengering over some souvenirs from tonight's game. Run `em all through forensics and get back to me ASAP."

"Okay, Jake. As soon as it arrives, I'll walk it down myself." He paused. "And boss—try to get some rest. You sound exhausted."

Jake hung up and placed his PDA back inside his blazer pocket. As he did, Krycerick approached and placed his hand on Jake's shoulder.

"You look tired, Deputy Director."

Jake frowned, "Yeah, so I've been told."

"Well, I'm pretty much done here," said Krycerick as he glanced at his watch. "We still have an hour and a half to go before Detective Sagiv shows up with the football team. When was the last time you ate anything?"

Jake shrugged. "Breakfast." He paused and thought for a moment. "Breakfast yesterday."

Krycerick chuckled. "Come on then, Jake. I'll buy you a steak sandwich. I know a great place."

Although Jake would have preferred sticking around the crime scene to sort through some of the pieces of the puzzle, his pounding head was getting worse and he knew that if he didn't eat something soon he would be useless. "Okay, Chief, as long as you're buying," he said, as the two men headed for the door and exited the locker room.

CHAPTER 17

THE ARTIST'S HEAD WAS SPINNING with excitement, and he could feel the adrenaline pulsating through his veins as he turned off Sunset Boulevard and drove slowly through the parking lot of his motel. He pulled behind the main building and brought his car to a stop beside a large green trash bin that was surrounded by a rusty chain link fence. There was an even rustier sign hanging from a broken gate that read, 'No illegal dumping—Violators will be prosecuted.'

It was a darker than usual night with no moon in the sky, and the few lampposts that actually worked did little to illuminate the parking lot. Cautiously, he checked in all directions to make sure no one was watching. *As usual, he was completely alone.* Besides a few other guests who were mostly alcoholics and junkies, The Artist pretty much had the entire place to himself. Once he was absolutely certain the coast was clear, he reached over the seat, grabbed a large black garbage bag containing the custodian's uniform he had worn earlier, and got out of the car. Using both hands, he swung the bag behind his body and then launched it over the fence into the center of the trash bin. He let out a loud cackle. "Two points," he crowed. He got back into his car, pulled into his assigned space, and made his way up the concrete steps to his room.

Completely out of breath, The Artist searched his pockets for the key, but it was nowhere to be found. *Probably still in the uniform trousers,* he thought. Then he noticed the cardboard the landlord had secured over the broken window, and he smiled.

Once safely inside his room, The Artist switched on the television and began surfing through the channels. He took a seat on the corner of his unmade sofa bed and reached for an open pack of smokes on the nightstand. He slid the last Marlboro Light from the pack and placed it between his lips. He lit the cigarette, inhaled the smoke deep into his lungs and then exhaled a stream of smoke through his nostrils like an angry bull.

As he had expected, every station was now reporting on the brutal slaying of superstar quarterback Trevor Hash. Fox News was live from outside the LA Coliseum and the word 'Exclusive' was flashing across the bottom of his TV in red letters. The artist took a long drag on his cigarette and turned up the volume on the TV.

"This is Dede Erickson reporting from outside the LA Coliseum, where earlier this evening the killer that many are now calling the Shapiro Slayer struck again. This time, the victim is USC quarterback Trevor Hash who had just won his fifth consecutive game of the season against the Notre Dame Fighting Irish."

A photo of Trevor was now displayed at the top of the screen. He was smiling and wearing a dark blue suit with an open collar—probably taken from the USC yearbook.

"Sources say that the killer used the same weapon as he did in the previous night's murder at the home of actress

Brooklyn Sims." The reporter briefly glanced down at her note card. "*A straight-edged blade, most likely a sword or a machete.*"

The photo of Trevor was now replaced with a picture of the Academy Award. It had been photo shopped by someone at Fox News to read Shapiro Talent Agency across its base.

"*Left behind, the killer's signature: a small replica of the Academy Award, with an inscription on the pedestal—Shapiro Talent Agency.*"

The Artist smiled as he took a final drag on his cigarette and flicked it through the hole in the wall. It ricocheted off the railing causing sparks to fly in all directions before falling into the murky swimming pool below. He stood from the bed and arched his back in a stretch as he lowered the volume on the television and made his way into the kitchen. He knew that he had done well tonight, extremely well, and he knew that he would be commended for it. He glanced down at his PDA on the kitchen table. *No messages.* "Still too soon," he mumbled to himself as he slid open a drawer, pulled out a bottle of pills and poured an assortment into his mouth. He opened the refrigerator and pulled out a can of beer, took a big swig and washed down the medicine. He then shot one more glance at his PDA that still indicated no messages and walked back into the living room.

"Well, well, well, what have we here?" cackled The Artist as he raised the volume on the television. Then he grinned. "And all along I thought you were too superior to give interviews, Deputy Director."

"*This is Dede Erickson and I have here with me FBI Deputy Director Jake Chase.*" She paused and looked up at Jake, who stood nearly a foot taller than her. *"Deputy Director, why has the FBI taken an interest in these murders?"*

Jake looked angry. *"The FBI hasn't taken an interest . . . I have"* he said through clenched teeth.

The reporter appeared confused. *"I don't understand, Deputy Director."* She paused. *"Did you say the FBI isn't investigating these two murders?"*

"No," replied Jake. *"I am. The killer has made this personal."* Then he looked at the camera. *"You wanted my attention? Now you've got it . . . one hundred percent of it!"* His voice was deliberate. *"But let me tell you this,"* he said, as he pointed his finger at the camera. *"You have made a powerful enemy today, my friend!"*

The reporter let out a slight gasp and then caught her breath as she regained her composure. *"This is Dede Erickson, reporting to you live from the LA Coliseum."*

The Artist was motionless as he silently stared down at the TV. Inadvertently, his grip loosened and the can of beer fell to the floor, spilling out onto the carpet. "Fuck!" He screamed as he quickly made his way to the nightstand. "Don't let him get into your head," he said, as he forced open the drawer and pulled out a 9mm semi-automatic and a silencer. He took a deep breath. "Get it together, man. He's just fucking with you," he muttered nervously as he screwed the silencer into the barrel of the gun and placed it on the nightstand. "Sleep, that's all, I just need to get some sleep," he said, as he turned off the television with the remote and hit the switch on the small lamp beside the bed. The room fell dark and he could feel the meds starting to kick in. Slowly, he slumped back onto the bed and rested his head on the pillow. He could still faintly smell her scent and it made him smile. He looked over at the small alarm clock: *10:05 p.m.* A few hours of sleep were all he needed, and then he would head to Vegas.

CHAPTER 18

GIANNAS WAS A HOT NEW RESTAURANT in downtown Los Angeles that had recently opened its doors but was already receiving rave reviews for its art deco decor, fabulous food and over-the-top cocktail menu, boasting 15 different types of mojitos. The clientele ranged from USC college students and professors to Hollywood celebrities, movers and shakers. Although *Giannas* was always packed, the restaurant didn't take reservations.

The owner and namesake, Gianna, had graduated from The Culinary Institute of America several years ago and now handled everything from meeting and greeting customers to preparing some of the restaurant's incredible desserts. Gianna was a beautiful, successful businesswoman—and she happened to be Eddie "Nails" Krycerick's only daughter.

Jake and Chief Krycerick entered the crowded restaurant and made their way across the room to the hostess station, where an attractive black woman stood behind a steel podium, scribbling down names in a leather bound ledger. She was wearing a form-fitting red dress that set her apart from the other servers in the restaurant who all wore black. The moment she spotted the two men approaching, a huge smile came across her face. "Hey, Nails," she said excitedly as she made her way around the podium and kissed him on the cheek.

She lingered by his ear for a moment. "Who's your cute friend?" she whispered.

Krycerick smiled and took a step back, positioning himself between the hostess and Jake. "Shari Rubin, I'd like you to meet Jake Chase," he said, nodding in Jake's direction.

Jake smiled and extended his hand.

Shari's eyes widened as she brought her hand to her mouth. "You're that FBI guy," she said, pointing to one of the plasmas hanging on the wall behind the bar. "The whole restaurant just watched you on the news." She appeared smitten. "I have to tell you, you gave me goose bumps."

Jake's smile suddenly vanished as he lowered his hand to his side. He looked at Krycerick and frowned.

Krycerick cleared his throat. "Shari, is Gianna around?"

"Uh-huh." Shari nodded, still staring at Jake. Slowly she shifted her attention to Krycerick as if coming out of a weird trance. "Sorry, Nails. Yeah, she's in her office, go on back."

Krycerick looked over the crowded restaurant and then back at Jake. "Grab us a couple seats in the lounge. I'm just gonna go say hello."

Jake nodded. "Sure." He gave a polite smile to Shari and then made his way to the lounge. As he did, he could hear Shari thanking Krycerick for helping her get a part in some Quentin Tarantino movie. The statement made Jake pause for a moment. It struck him as odd and completely out of character for Chief Krycerick, but really, what did he actually know about this man with a long and complicated history? He shrugged it off and took a seat at the corner of the bar.

The lounge at *Giannas* was packed as usual. Much like the dining room, it was handsomely decorated, with a long copper-topped bar running the length of the room. Scattered about, in no particular arrangement, were an assortment of pastel colored fabric couches where patrons were relaxing and enjoying the restaurant's signature mojitos. Behind the bar, fluorescent lights cast a soothing hue over a mirrored wall in front of which stood a multitude of tequila bottles of various shapes and sizes. The effect was interesting, to say the least.

Jake looked down at the far end of the bar where three men were downing shots of whiskey and falling over one another. They appeared to be in their early 20s and were all visibly intoxicated, laughing and making crude comments about certain parts of one of the waitress's anatomy. They were all wearing jeans and T-shirts and their short, cropped hair was covered by black baseball caps worn backwards. They certainly didn't fit in with the rest of the well-dressed customers in the lounge, and Jake wondered what they were doing there.

"Hi there, my name is Stacy and welcome to *Giannas*," said one of the bartenders, smiling over the bar at Jake. "Sorry for the wait, there are only two of us on tonight, and we're pretty busy." She glanced over at the other female bartender, who was desperately trying to get control of the three obnoxious guys, and frowned. She turned back to Jake. "Can I interest you in a mojito?"

Jake shook his head, wincing as he did so. The headache was still there. "Sam Adams . . . and a menu."

"You got it. Bottle of Sam and a . . ." she paused. "Hey, don't I know you from somewhere?"

Jake grimaced and then forced a slight smile. "I don't think so."

Stacy tapped her finger against her lips, considering. "Okay," she said slowly, "if you say so." She turned and headed down the long bar and stopped in front of a small, glass-paneled refrigerator that was filled with rows and rows of various types of bottled beer. She leaned over, pulled open the glass door, and reached for a bottle of Sam Adams. Before she could stand up, however, one of the obnoxious guys at the end of the bar hauled back and whacked her on her ass so hard that Jake could hear the smacking sound from where he was sitting.

Stacy let out a loud yelp and jumped. As she did, the bottle of beer fell from her hand and smashed to pieces on the tile floor. The loud noise caused everyone in the lounge to turn and stare. She gasped in exasperation and the three men began cracking up. "Assholes," she mumbled under her breath as she knelt to pick up the shards of broken glass.

Jake watched silently. His head was pounding, but now it had nothing to do with food or sleep; now it was fueled by pure anger for the three men at the end of the bar. He clenched his hands into tight fists, slowly stood and walked over to the three men. They were still laughing and falling into one another as they gulped down shots of Jack Daniels and slammed the glasses down onto the bar. As Jake approached, he noticed something very interesting about all three men. Each had a small blue teardrop tattooed under his left eye. It was a gang identifier. Under the left eye, it meant you were a Blood or part of the Peoples Nation. Under the right eye, it meant you were a Crip or part of the Folk Nation. Rival gangs; a person with a tear on the left would never be seen with a person with a tear on the right. When the two met, it usually meant that someone would end up dead.

"Something funny, ladies?" Jake asked angrily through clenched teeth.

Suddenly, the three men stopped laughing and turned to face Jake. They all had a look of astonishment. "What the fuck did you just say, homie?"

Jake took a step closer, positioning himself in front of all three men, but spoke to the man who had smacked Stacy. His voice was quiet but deliberate. "Here's the deal . . . homie. The way I see it, you've got two choices." He nodded at Stacy who was watching Jake in disbelief. "You can apologize to my friend, pay your bill and get the fuck out of here."

Stacy smiled.

"Or what, punk ass?"

Jake grinned. "Or the four of us can go outside and I can teach you boys a little lesson in manners." He made eye contact with each of them. "Now, you guys think you got the horses for that?"

"Get the fuck outta here," barked one of the men as he reached forward and gave Jake a shove on the shoulder. Jake didn't budge. In fact, the blow forced the man's hand to snap backwards—and a look of dismay appeared on his face. Then he noticed Jake's gun strapped into his shoulder holster under his blazer. "He's got a piece," shouted the man.

The gang's leader let out a laugh. "You wouldn't be so badass without that gat, homeboy," he mocked. Then he looked from side to side at the other men. "I knew it," he continued. "He ain't nuttin' but a . . ."

Before the man could finish, Jake reached inside his blazer, unclipped his Glock from the shoulder holster and pulled the weapon out. He pressed a small lever and the clip slid out and fell to the floor with a loud clanking sound. He racked the chamber and a single bullet sprung from the top of the gun and fell to the ground and rolled under a bar stool. He slammed the gun down hard onto the bar and turned his palms to the ceiling. "Your move, tough guy."

For a brief moment, the man seemed stunned, but then reeled back and swung hard at Jake's head. Quickly, Jake leaned back allowing the blow to pass by his face. He then grabbed the man's arm and swung him around fast so that the thug was now facing his two cronies as Jake forced the heel of his foot into the back of the man's leg. The man crumpled to the ground, and Jake immediately pinned his head to the floor with his foot. Without wasting a second, Jake grabbed the other two guys by the back of their heads, and before they could react, he smashed their faces together. He then spun one of the men around and brought him to his knees, holding him in a tight headlock as he slammed the third man's head into the bar, holding it tightly in place facing Stacy, who appeared to be in shock. He sighed. "Now, like I was saying, we can do this the easy way and you can simply apologize, or we can do it the hard way."

"Whoa!" exclaimed Stacy, shaking her head in disbelief. Then she looked at Jake and smiled as she mouthed the words *thank you.*

"You motherfucker," screamed a fourth gang member, who was charging at full speed in Jake's direction with a switchblade held high over his head. "I'm gonna fucking kill you, motherfucker!"

Suddenly, a huge arm extended across the screaming man's path and clothes-lined him across the neck. The man's feet flew out from underneath him and shot into the air as his head crashed to the floor with an earth-shattering thud.

Chief Krycerick lowered his arm and shrugged at Jake. "I mean, I know you didn't need any help, but I couldn't resist." He looked down at the unconscious man and shook his head. "Fucking gangbangers."

Just then, Jake's cell went off. He let out a huff as he stomped down on the man's head, which was still pinned under his foot, and tightened the pressure on the man in the head lock and the other who was face down on the bar, causing each to grunt and moan in agony. He looked over at Stacy. "Would you mind?" he asked, nodding to his pocket.

She looked at him curiously, "I don't understand."

Jake nodded to his pocket again. "My phone. Would you mind grabbing it and holding it to my ear?"

"Oh, um, sure," she replied, as she reached over the man's head and into Jake's pocket. She glanced down at the caller ID. "It says Diane."

Jake smiled. "It's the wife." He looked at Stacy. "Just hit the green button and hold it against my ear." He then gave another shove down on the three men as he angled his ear against the PDA. "Hi honey."

"Hi Jake, how's it going?"

Jake looked around the room. Although most of the customers had cleared out, those who remained were all staring at him in amazement. "Oh, you know LA."

"Yeah, I saw you on the news." She paused. "You look tired."

"Oh, probably just the time difference."

"Okay, if you say so, but try to get some rest, baby." A brief silence. "Oh yeah, great news, I got someone to fill in for me at Blythedale, so I'm gonna fly out Sunday. Can you meet me at the airport?"

Just then, the guy Krycerick had knocked out was starting to regain consciousness, but as he started to get up, Krycerick gave him another blow to the head with a closed fist and he was out again.

"Sure honey, sounds great."

"Okay," replied Diane. "See you Sunday night . . . oh, and Jake"

"Yeah, honey?"

"Be careful."

"Always," he said, and then nodded to Stacy to take the phone. Again, he tightened his grip on the two men and stomped down harder with his foot. "Okay, fellas, who wants to apologize first?"

It was almost 10:30 by the time Jake and Krycerick were seated in the dining room at Giannas. Eddie was working on a seltzer with a slice of lime and Jake was rolling an ice-cold bottle of Sam Adams across his brow, hoping for some relief from his pounding head. The earlier disturbance didn't seem to have much of an effect on the still-very-crowded restaurant. In fact, seated at the next table were Russell Crowe and Colin Farrell. Jake brought the bottle to his mouth and took a big swig. As he did, he noticed that Russell Crowe was staring at him. Crowe then raised his bottle of Heineken and tilted in it Jake's direction. "Good on ya, mate."

Jake forced a smile and then turned back to Krycerick. "Pride," he said. "That's the common denominator here, pride." He then brought his hand to the back of his neck and tried to squeeze out some of the tension. He tilted his head from side to side as he squeezed tighter, but it was no use.

Krycerick shook his head. "I'm not following ya."

"I'm not talking about when your kid hits a home run, pride. I'm talking about an over-the-top sense of self worth." Jake shook his head and took another sip of beer. "Ya know, like 90 percent of the people out here. Brooklyn Sims, Lefty Shapiro, even Trevor Hash. Egomaniacs, all of them and I think that's what pisses this guy off." He ran his fingers through his hair, combing it back off his brow. "Probably why he decapitates them."

Krycerick nodded as he looked around the restaurant. Two leggy blonds with huge fake boobs had giggled their way into a conversation with Farrell and Crowe. He took a sip of his seltzer. "The Roman Catholic Church lists pride as the most deadly of the seven sins."

Jake shot him a grin. "Catholic school, right?"

Krycerick laughed. "Yeah, Catholic school." Then he reached for his wallet and flipped open to a picture of his son, Matthew. He slid the photo out of a clear plastic holder and handed it across the table to Jake. "But I majored in philosophy." His voice was more serious now. "Aristotle considered pride a profound virtue." He paused. "Do you have kids, Jake?"

Jake looked down at the photograph of Krycerick's son. He was a handsome young man dressed in Army fatigues. His hair was cut short, and he was the spitting image of his father in younger days, with a squared off jaw-line and boyish good looks. "Nice looking boy," Jake said, as he handed the photo back to Krycerick.

"He's a captain in the Army," replied Krycerick, and his eyes lingered on the photo a few extra seconds before replacing it into the plastic holder. He took a breath and looked across at Jake. "So, no kids, Deputy Director?"

Jake shook his head. He didn't feel like getting too personal with the Chief, and he really didn't feel like discussing Diane and the twins when he needed to be focused on the business at hand.

"Here ya go, gentlemen. Two steak sandwiches," interrupted one of the waitresses as she set a plate in front of each of the men. She smiled. "Can I get you anything else?"

"I think we're okay for now," replied Krycerick, as he reached for a large onion ring and stuffed it in his mouth.

"Okay, Nails. Just call me if you need anything."

Jake took another swig from his beer and leaned into the table. "Look, I think we need to pay another visit to Lefty Shapiro in the morning. Take a look at his client list and see if we can't figure out some kind of a pattern here."

Krycerick nodded his head as he took a big bite out of his steak sandwich. "You think he'll be working on a Sunday?"

Jake shrugged. "Who knows, but that agency seems to tie this whole thing together somehow." He slid the plate to the side. "I want Brooklyn Sims in protective custody ASAP."

Krycerick put the sandwich back down on the plate. "She's gone into hiding, Jake. No one can locate her."

Jake let out a slight chuckle as he reached for his cell phone. He pressed the speed dial button for Michael Jarvis and within seconds he was on the line.

"Hey boss, what's up?"

"Mike, I want you to track down Brooklyn Sims."

"You got it, Jake."

"Have a field team bring her in and call me as soon as it happens."

"Consider it done."

Jake hung up the phone and placed it down on the table in front of him. He reached for his beer, gulped back the final sip and looked over at Krycerick. "Wanna get out of here?"

Krycerick was just about to take another bite from his sandwich. "Sure," he said, as he closed his mouth and put the sandwich back on the plate. He rubbed his hands together in an abbreviated clapping motion brushing the crumbs onto his plate and then stood up. "Let me ask you a question, Jake. How do you plan on finding Brooklyn Sims? I mean, these celebrities, when they don't want . . . ."

Jake smiled and turned his palms up. "Nails, we're the FBI. We found Saddam Hussein in a tiny cellar in a farmhouse 15 kilometers south of Tikrit, I think we can find Brooklyn Sims."

CHAPTER 19

BROOKLYN SIMS MADE HER WAY ACROSS the terracotta floor in the 15 thousand dollar-a-night Spanish style casita she had rented at the Desert Mountain Spa in Palm Springs. The tile felt cool under her bare feet, and the slight breeze from the ceiling fans picked up the scent of jasmine in the air and created a warm, tranquil feeling throughout the small, candle-lit room.

Escaping the stresses of LA had indeed turned out to be the right thing to do. She needed to get away from it all and clear her mind for a while. She had only been there a day, and already she was feeling much better.

The exclusive spa only permitted 20 guests to stay at the same time and maintained a very strict policy against the use of cell phones in public areas; calls were restricted to the guest's suite. Brooke hadn't even turned hers on. The entire resort was devoid of any land lines, televisions, radios and newspapers. Guests were essentially cut off from the world, and Brooke couldn't have been happier. The only person who knew she was there was her sister Doreen, who knew not to bother her unless there was a real emergency.

The horrifying image of Skyler's headless body was still embedded in her memory and probably would be for a long, long time, but what could you expect? With the type of people Skyler choose to hang out with, her death wasn't all too surprising. At least that's what Brooke told herself.

Brooke sighed and tried hard to erase the gruesome image from her memory, but it was no use. She could hear Lefty's voice echoing in her head, *that chick is bad news, kid!* She shuddered and made her way in the direction of the lanai. The large sliding doors were open, covered only by sheer white curtains that danced eerily in a ghostly fashion, in and out of the room. Brooke headed for the middle, found the seam in the fabric and stepped out onto the balcony. The warm night air felt nice on her face as she took a deep breath and gazed up at the dark sky, peppered with millions of tiny bright stars, something she truly missed living in smog-covered LA. She leaned on the railing and looked out over the desert. Her breath steadied and she felt much calmer now. Tomorrow she would soak all day long in the mineral pool, lay carelessly in the warm desert sun, eat wonderful exotic chilled fruits, and then go for a deep-tissue massage. The thought of it made her smile. But just as she was approaching a Zen-like state, the image of Skyler Dawn's body reappeared in her mind's eye. This time she thought about her conversation with that FBI guy, Jake Chase. Something he had said had been bothering her all day. At first, she blew it off, but what if he was right? What if the killer hadn't been there looking for Sky and had actually come for her? But why? Who would want to hurt her? She felt her heart begin to race as thoughts of poolside protein shakes were quickly replaced by fear and anxiety. The howl of a coyote in the distance startled her out of her thoughts. She frowned. "I need a cigarette," she said, as she turned and made her way back into the house. She grabbed her purse from the couch and began rifling through it. Suddenly, she heard a noise coming from the front of the casita. It was the sound of the front door squeaking on its hinges and then closing shut. Someone was now in the house with her! Brooke could feel her heart begin to pound against her chest as she accidently dropped her bag. For a moment, she stared down at the floor, wondering if whoever it was in the next room had just heard the sound the bag made as it crashed against the tiles. She took a breath and slowly began to make her way in the direction of the intruder. She could hear footsteps approaching the long hallway that connected the two rooms and was completely frozen with fear as thoughts of Skyler Dawn and Jake Chase raced through her brain. She squinted against the darkness and could see a shadow quickly walking toward her.

"Can I help you?" she called out into the darkness, the sound of fear apparent in her voice.

"There you are! I've been looking all over for you."

Confusion and relief flooded Brooke's face. "Doreen?"

Brooke's sister smiled. "You know, you really should lock your front door." She placed her overnight bag on the floor by her feet, walked up to Brooke and gave her a peck on the cheek.

Brooke was dumfounded. "Doreen, what are you doing here? Is everything okay? Is it Mom?"

From a distance, the sisters were the spitting image of one another; same height, same weight, same hair color and style, and although Doreen Sims was attractive in her own right, she didn't possess the striking features that made her sister jump off the movie screen. She didn't have the high cheekbones or the captivating eyes that Brooke had, and it was those attributes that made Brooklyn Sims a Hollywood superstar and Doreen Sims a Modesto real estate agent.

Doreen chuckled. "Mom's fine," she replied as she placed the backs of her hands on her hips and gazed around the room. She nodded her head approvingly. "Must be nice," she muttered.

Brooke was growing impatient. "Doreen, please! I'm a little on edge." Her voice was more deliberate now. "What are you doing here? I told you I only wanted to be contacted if there was an emergency."

"I know, baby sister," replied Doreen. Then she made her way back to her overnight bag. "I tried calling all day but your phone went straight to voice-mail." She knelt down in front of the bag, drew back the zipper and pulled out two bottles of wine and her iPod.

Brooke glanced over at her cell phone on the coffee table where she had left it earlier that day. She then turned back to her sister. "I don't understand."

Doreen placed both bottles on a small table beside the sofa. She handed the iPod over to Brooke and hit play. "I thought you might want to see this," she said.

Brooke looked at her sister quizzically then gazed down at the small LCD panel. It was a video from one of the news reports earlier that evening regarding the Trevor Hash murder. She watched in shock as a reporter, standing in front of the LA Coliseum, detailed the horrific incident. Across the bottom of the screen in red letters were the words SHAPIRO SLAYER STRIKES AGAIN!

Brooke brought her hand to her mouth. "Oh no," she said in a muted voice as she continued watching. "They think he's going after Lefty's clients." She looked back at Doreen. Her face was stricken with fear and disbelief.

"Yeah, some FBI guy says the killer was looking for you last night but got the wrong person by mistake."

"Jake Chase," murmured Brooke.

Doreen paused and tilted her head sideways. "Yeah, how'd you know that?"

Brooke handed the iPod back to her sister and began rummaging through her bag again. "He's not just some FBI agent, Doreen." She stopped. "Do you have a cigarette?"

Doreen shook her head. "I quit a year and a half ago."

"Right," replied Brooke, sounding annoyed, and then resumed her search, this time by dumping the entire contents of her purse onto the couch. "Anyway, he's the deputy director, you know, that guy from Paramount last summer."

Doreen's eyes widened. "Oh my God, I knew he looked familiar." Then she smiled.

"What?" asked Brooke, who had given up her search for a cigarette and grabbed one of the bottles of wine instead.

"Nothing," replied Doreen. "It's just that . . . have you seen this guy, Brooke?" She paused. "I mean, he's tall, dark and really rugged looking—and you should hear him." She shook her head. "He means business all right, and he really wants to protect you from this guy."

Brooke pulled the cork from the bottle and filled two large wine glasses. She took a big gulp from one and then handed the other to Doreen. "So, what, I'm supposed to be happy about this?"

Doreen drank then set her glass down. "No, of course not. It's just that he's the real deal. Not like those poser actors from your movies." She stopped and a serious look came over her face. "Brooksie, I think for whatever reason this Shapiro slayer guy is after you, you got lucky last night. Next time you might not be so lucky."

Brooke stayed silent. She finished off her wine and poured herself another glass. She walked to the couch and looked down at the contents of her purse scattered about the cushions. She sighed, then reached down and grabbed the card Jake had given her the night before. "Okay, Jake Chase. I just hope you're the hero everyone seems to think you are."

CHAPTER 20

AT 11:00 P.M. SHARP, JAKE WAS STANDING in front of the USC locker room with the entire football team, coaches, directors and team physician assembled down the long corridor in front of him. Standing beside him were Chief Krycerick, Dr. Bonina and a few detectives from the LAPD. The media frenzy outside the Coliseum had quadrupled, as the recent events became worldwide news. Network news as well as representatives from all the major cable stations had joined local media. The mayor had imposed a 9:00 p.m. curfew and the entire Hollywood community was paralyzed with fear, especially those represented by the Shapiro Agency.

Jake looked down the long hallway at the solemn faces that stood before him. The expressions spoke volumes of the fear and sadness they felt. He was just about to speak when something caught his eye, a small, red, flashing light at the end of the hallway just above the exit sign. It was a surveillance camera. *Why hadn't he seen it before?* He leaned over to Chief Krycerick, pointed to the small flashing light and whispered in his ear. "Find out where that feeds."

Krycerick nodded and quickly exited the corridor for the main campus building.

Jake cleared his throat. "Gentleman, my name is Jake Chase. I am the Deputy Director of the Federal

Bureau of Investigation." He suddenly had everyone's undivided attention, and all eyes looked to him for answers. "I know this horrific incident comes as a huge shock to you all, and I want you to know that the local authorities, with the help of the FBI, are doing everything in their power to keep you safe and bring a swift end to these killings." The room was silent. "Now," Jake continued, "we are going to be conducting interviews with all of you starting tomorrow morning at 7:00 a.m. in the main reading room at the Doheny Library. The interviews will take no more than 15 minutes of your time. Please be prompt." He nodded at one of the detectives. "Detective Sagiv will give you your allotted time slot. That is all."

Jake turned and started in the direction of the locker room as Detective Sagiv began calling out players' names and the designated times. Dr. Bonina placed her hand on Jake's shoulder, allowing it to linger for a moment.

"Jake, you look exhausted," she said with a look of concern. "Why not get some rest? We'll start fresh in the morning." She removed her hand from his shoulder and glanced over at Detective Sagiv. "Maybe we'll catch a break and one these kids will have seen something."

Just then a shadow fell over both of them. "Mr. Chase, my name is Marc Sanzeri. I play ball for USC and Trevor Hash was my best friend."

Jake turned to see the enormous lineman towering over him. His eyes were red and he had been crying.

"What can I do for you, son?" replied Jake.

Sanzeri reached into his pocket and pulled out a key. It was attached to a dark blue, oval shaped piece of plastic by a small metal ring and had the number 314 written on either side. Below the numbers was a black silhouette of a king's crown. "I found this in front of my locker. I think it's a room key."

Jake took the key from Sanzeri. He looked at both sides of the plastic holder. There was only a room number and the crown silhouette with no indication of which hotel it had come from. "When did you find this?"

The big lineman put both hands in his front pockets. He was visibly upset. "Just after the game." He paused. His voice was shaky. "I didn't think much of it. I mean, we're always gettin' stuff like that. You know, the fans . . . the booster club." He shook his head. "Hell, I just figured it was some rally girl lookin' to get a little." A look of embarrassment came across his face and glanced over at Dr. Bonina. "Sorry, ma'am."

Bonina was unfazed. She turned to Jake. "What do ya think?"

Jake shrugged his shoulders. "Dunno, could be something, could be nothing. Let's get it to Krycerick's people and see if we can't find out which hotel it's from."

Bonina took the key from Jake and ran her finger along its spiky teeth. "Motel, Jake, probably an old one at that."

"What's that?" replied Jake.

Bonina handed the key back to Jake. "It's from one of the older motels. There's a bunch of them along Sunset. You can check, but I'm pretty sure all of the hotels in the city, and most of the newer motels, have switched to magnetic keys."

Jake gave her a nod then glanced over at Sanzeri. "Okay, good work, son. Now why don't you go join your team and find out your assignment for tomorrow?"

"Okay, Mr. Chase, I hope it helps," replied Sanzeri as he turned and walked toward Detective Sagiv.

Just then, Jake's cell phone went off. It was Krycerick. "Yeah, Chief, whaddya got?"

"Jake, I'm at the USC Department of Public Safety. All campus video surveillance feeds here and we've got some pretty interesting footage."

"Okay, I'm on my way," replied Jake, as he hung up the phone and placed it into his blazer pocket. "Krycerick's got something," he said to Bonina as he handed her the room key. "Give this to Sagiv and tell him to find out exactly where it's from and send a few men to investigate. We'll touch base tomorrow."

Jake pulled open the glass door and entered the Department of Public Safety. The DPS was one of the largest university law enforcement departments in the United States and employed hundreds of full-time staff.

It was nearly midnight, and on any other Saturday evening there might have been 20 or 30 security personnel on duty. Tonight, all employees were working overtime, mostly answering calls from frantic parents who had been unsuccessful in contacting their kids on their cell phones.

Jake approached the front desk where one of the student volunteers was busy talking into a headset. Stenciled on the wall behind her were the words "We Cultivate Talent and Protect USC's Assets." The young woman was trying her best to reassure some nervous parent that the University had the situation well under control and that her son was perfectly safe. She hung up the phone, removed the headset, and looked up at Jake. "How can I help you?" she asked.

Jake reached into his back pocket and pulled his ID from his wallet. "I'm Deputy Director Jake Chase," he said, holding out his identification. "I'm here to see Chief Krycerick."

"Back here, Jake," Krycerick called from the next room.

The woman smiled and placed the headset back over her ear.

As Jake made his way around the corner, he couldn't believe his eyes. The entire place was buzzing with activity. Local law enforcement agents were scattered about speaking to campus security officers, and it seemed as though every phone in the entire place was ringing at once. Anyone who wasn't busy with the LAPD was on a headset assuring whoever was on the other end that the DPS had the situation well under control. Jake wondered if that was actually a true statement.

Krycerick was standing outside the door to one of the offices that was situated in each of the corners of the large room. He nodded as Jake approached. "How'd it go back at the Coliseum?"

"We may have caught a break," replied Jake. "Some kid found a motel room key in front of his locker."

"You think it belongs to the killer?"

Jake shrugged. "Or a rally girl." He looked past Krycerick into the office. "What's going on in here?"

"DPS video surveillance room," replied the Chief. He gestured into the office with his thumb. "Come on in, Jake. I think you're gonna be happy with what we found."

The two men entered the large office and made their way to a huge flat screen monitor, nearly 6 feet in diameter, mounted on the wall. In front of it was a desk on which sat three more monitors, all displaying various areas around USC. Every few seconds the video feed on each would flash to another section on campus. The entire room was filled with desks and monitors all silently patrolling the entire university. It was quite impressive.

"Jake, I'd like you to meet USC Security Chief Aaron Depass," said Krycerick, motioning to a tall, good-looking black man who was standing inches from the large screen and seemed to be studying something with great concentration. Three other men, all of whom seemed just as interested on what was displayed on the flat panel, accompanied him.

Depass turned to Jake and extended his hand. "Deputy Director, it's a pleasure to meet you. I've read a lot about you."

Although Depass was nearing 50, he was in terrific shape, typical ex-marine. A thin mustache just above his lip gave him a distinguished look and contrasted with his shaved head.

Jake shook the man's hand then pointed to the monitor. It was now showing the corridor in front of the locker room and, from the vantage point currently displayed, Jake figured it was from the feed off the camera he had spotted above the exit sign. "What can you tell me about this, Mr. Depass?"

Depass smiled and walked up to the monitor. "Let me show you," he said, as he placed his finger on the screen causing a date and time display to appear at the top corner of the monitor. It read *Sunday, 12:46.32a.m.*—the current time.

Jake looked at his watch and frowned.

Along the bottom of the panel was a group of arrows—one pointing left, one right, and a larger arrow pointing up, under which was the word *PLAY.*

Depass pressed the arrow pointing left and the clock sprung to life, quickly counting backwards. He moved to the side of the screen and turned to face Jake and Krycerick. "Okay, gentlemen, here is the feed from this afternoon." He stopped rewinding at exactly 4:22.00p.m. The image revealed the long, empty hallway in front of the locker room. "Okay, no one around. Not too unusual, especially during a big game like the one today." He hit the play arrow and the clock began moving forwards; 4:22.01, 4:22.02, 4:22.03, 4:22.04 . . . .

At 4:22.13 a man appeared. He had entered from a point below the camera and proceeded down the long hallway in the direction of the locker room. Jake could see only the man's back as he entered the locker room and disappeared from the camera's eye. He had been wearing what appeared to be a beige-colored custodian's uniform, and Jake didn't see anything out of the ordinary.

"We now have over 500 surveillance cameras throughout the campus, all pretty well hidden," said Depass. He then placed his thumb and index finger from both hands on the image of the door to the locker room. He drew his fingers apart in an outward motion causing the image of the door to zoom in. He did this several times until the image was so close Jake could actually read the words *Trojans SC Locker Room—Pass Required*. "Of course, there are some places cameras aren't permitted," he continued.

Krycerick leaned over to Jake and smiled. "Watch this."

Depass placed his finger on the arrow pointing right and the video began fast-forwarding. He stopped it at 4:34.14 and then hit *play*.

Jake watched as the locker room door swung open and the man in the custodian's uniform walked out. Depass froze the video and zoomed in tighter on the man's face.

Jake looked at Krycerick quizzically. "I don't get it."

Krycerick chuckled. "You'll see," he replied.

Depass walked around to the desk in front of the wall monitor and typed something onto the keyboard. The image of the custodian's face was now displayed on one of the desktop monitors. He then made his way back to the wall and once again pressed the fast-forward icon. This time he stopped the feed at 7:22.46. The image of the door was still on the screen as he pressed *play*. Again, Jake watched as the locker room door swung open and the same man in the custodian's uniform proceeded through, but this time he was carrying a large green duffel and this time he appeared to have blood on his face and shirt. With a few keystrokes, the man's face appeared on the second desktop monitor.

Jake approached the desk and stared down at the two images frozen on the monitors. He was looking at the face of a killer, his killer. He turned to Depass. "Have you sent this to LAPD?"

"Of course," replied Depass, as he walked up to the wall monitor for a third time. "But that's not all." This time he swept his hand across the entire length of the screen and, as he did so, the close-up of the killer's face was now replaced with the image of the same man approaching a car in the coliseum parking lot. The clock at the top of the screen had jumped to 7:34.32. Depass hit *play* and the three men watched as the killer got into a dark-colored Ford Taurus, backed the car from the spot, and drove out of the parking facility. Depass turned to

Jake. "Deputy Director, would you mind hitting *control* followed by the *F10* key, please."

As Jake did so, the image of the back of the car appeared on the third desktop monitor with the vehicle's license plate in full view. "Nice," Jake said, in a voice just above a whisper. He looked up at Depass. "I'm going to want a copy of this burned to . . ."

Before Jake could finish, Depass handed him two discs, each covered in white paper with the words *Personal & Confidential* written across the front in red letters. "Already made you copies, Deputy Director." Then he smiled at Krycerick. "I also e-mailed a copy to some guy named Jarvis at Quantico."

Jake grinned. He put his finger on the image of the killer's face. "Gotcha!"

CHAPTER 21

THE ARTIST WAS STARTLED BACK to consciousness by the sound of his BlackBerry vibrating and bouncing along the kitchen table in the next room. Slowly, he sat up in his bed and glanced at the clock. *1:15 a.m.* He twisted his neck from side to side, and made a loud crackling sound with each turn. He swung his feet onto the floor, grabbed his gun from the nightstand and headed for the kitchen where a small red light was flashing from his BlackBerry, briefly illuminating the dark room in a fluorescent red hue. He fell into a chair at the small kitchen table and reached for the device. There was a small envelope in the top corner of the screen indicating new mail. The Artist smiled. He knew it would be from her and he knew she would be pleased. He toggled to the small envelope and opened the e-mail.

Norris,

I love you so much. Tonight you were my hero. Have you turned on your television yet? The whole world is watching you, baby.

Just stick with the plan and soon they will know who you are and you will be famous.

I promise.

Norris Burns was The Artist's real name, although she was the only one who ever called him that. His stage name, the one on his Actors Guild card, was Burns

Newman. It just sounded better, more like the name of a Hollywood superstar. Indeed, he had played it over and over in his head a million times. *Ladies and gentlemen, this year's Oscar for best actor goes to . . . Burns Newman! Way to go Burns! Nice job Burnsie!*

Suddenly, the sound of a car's screeching tires somewhere off in the distance brought The Artist back to reality. He took a deep breath, and then reached for his cigarettes. He drew one from the box, threw it in his mouth and leaned over to the stove to light it. He exhaled a stream of smoke that loomed overhead like a dark rain cloud. He re-read the e-mail a second and third time, took another pull on his cigarette and then typed a response.

My Love,

I'm on my way to Las Vegas to take care of some music business. I will be back in LA tomorrow for Brooklyn Sims. Have you located her yet?

I can't believe we will be apart for six months—I don't know how I will survive without you.

The Artist sent the e-mail and exited the room. With his cigarette clenched between his teeth, he dragged a large red container from beneath the sofabed and set it upright on the floor in front of him. It was filled to the top with gasoline. Carefully, he unscrewed the cap and began splashing gasoline throughout the entire room. Once the container was empty, The Artist grabbed his duffel, stepped outside onto the walkway in front of his room, and took a final drag on his cigarette before flicking it back into the room.

With a loud whoosh the carpet was suddenly ablaze, and The Artist watched with a sadistic eagerness as the fire quickly spread from the floor to the curtains, to the bed and walls. Within seconds, the entire room was engulfed in flames, and he could feel the heat on his face as he tossed his duffel over his shoulder and made his way down the concrete steps to his car.

He could hear the sound of windows shattering and the loud wail of the fire alarms echoing throughout the building as the few guests staying at *The Emperor's Crown Motel* made their way down into the parking lot. Most of them appeared more annoyed by the inconvenience than worried about the blazing fire that was now quickly spreading through the motel.

The Artist flung his duffel into the back seat, shifted his Ford Taurus into drive and sped out of the parking lot. He glanced in the rearview mirror and could see thick black smoke billowing from the building as flames danced in every direction, illuminating the dark night sky.

"That ought to make the morning papers," he growled, as he headed along Sunset in the direction of the San Bernardino Freeway. And that was the important part, getting their attention so that they all knew who he was when he finally allowed them to catch him. He glanced down at the dashboard clock. It was just past 1:30 a.m. He knew that he could make it to Vegas in just over three hours, and, with any luck, he'd be back in LA by noon.

CHAPTER 22

JESSE AND HIS BROTHERS, ROBBIE AND LUKE, all downed their shots of whiskey and simultaneously slammed their glasses on top of the bar at *The Mint Hi-Limit Lounge,* located just off the main floor in the Palms hotel.

The Mint was a 5000 square foot, two-story VIP lounge with wood-paneled walls and marble mosaic floors, featuring no limit baccarat, blackjack, and roulette tables. There was also an adjoining poker room where high-stakes games that reached into the millions were rumored to have lasted for days. The second floor of The Mint featured an even more exclusive area to game, complete with views below and a private bar.

Jesse signaled to the cocktail waitress for another round. He was pumped, fueled by bourbon, adrenaline and youth. He felt completely unstoppable, like a locomotive going 100 miles an hour. And why shouldn't he? He was up 60 thousand at the craps tables, every chick in the place wanted to fuck him and every guy wanted to be him. He was a rock star and life was good.

"Here ya go, Jess," said the scantily clad waitress, as she set four shot glasses down on the bar in front of him. She had dark brown, shoulder length hair and was dressed in a pair of form-fitting, black slacks that left very little to the imagination and a black lace cami that barely covered her enormous fake boobs. She wore a diamond in her pierced navel and had a small tribal tattoo just above her waistline. She filled the four shot glasses to the rim and smiled at the three men. "This one's on me," she said as she raised one of the glasses head high. Jesse, Robbie and Luke all followed along and held their glasses in front of them.

"Vegas, baby!" shouted Luke as all four tilted their heads back and shot back the caramel colored liquid.

Again the three glasses hit the bar in unison as the three men hooted and hollered.

The waitress picked up the three empty shot glasses. "Thanks guys," she said as she retreated down the bar.

Jesse looked down at his watch. "When are we meeting up with Joey-G and Nicky?"

"'Bout an hour," replied Luke. "Ghostbar at 3:30."

Jesse nodded. He turned to face the casino and leaned his back against the bar. He was chewing on a thin cocktail straw, a habit he had picked up a long time ago. "This place is rockin" he said, as he scanned the large crowded room.

Everywhere he looked, attractive young women wearing barely any clothing were drinking fluorescent colored cocktails from oversized martini glasses. The gaming tables were all packed three deep with high rollers, and the casino made sure the room was filled with plenty of cold air, pure oxygen and loud music.

As Jessie gazed out over the casino floor, he spotted his personal casino host, Bethany, making her way across the crowded floor in the direction of the bar. Three beautiful women who all looked like models with their lacquered faces and teased hair accompanied her. They were escorts, and expensive ones at that.

Bethany worked for the casino, and it was her job to make sure that VIPs like Jesse, and certain high-rollers, more commonly known as whales, were afforded every possible amenity the hotel had to offer—and even some it didn't. Among the many items in her goodie bag, Bethany had access to fully comp'd private jets, hotel suites and villas, front-row tickets to shows that were sold out for months in advance, and always, a parting swag bag that often included Rolex watches and Cartier diamonds, just to keep them all coming back. Of course, in Jesse's case, the casino hosts had to be a bit more creative than dinner and a show. Although The Palms didn't permit prostitution on casino property, it was an unwritten rule that what two consenting adults (or three or four) did behind closed doors was their own business.

"Hi, guys," said Bethany, as she approached the group. "Having fun?" she asked, addressing all three men.

"Absolutely!" replied Robbie. "Hells yeah!" interjected Luke. Jesse just smiled, making eye contact with the three women standing behind Bethany.

"I hear you're up 60 grand, Jess. Congratulations."

"Yeah, something like that," replied Jessie halfheartedly, as he extended his hand to the woman who was closest to him. He smiled. "My name is Jesse James."

Bethany sighed and took a step back. *You guys are all the same.* She forced a smile and gestured to the three women. "Milena, Giselle and Sofia, I'd like you to meet Jesse James and his brothers, Luke and Robbie."

"Nice to meet you," replied the women, their voices heavy with Italian accents. "We love your music, Jesse," said Milena. "We listen to you all the time back in Milan."

Jesse smiled. "Thank you," he said appreciatively, although he knew enough to take the compliment lightly, considering its source. He knew very well that the three women standing before him were on the hotel's payroll, and that whether they liked his music or not, they were going to stroke his ego. And that included his host, Bethany. Fuck, he didn't even know for sure if they really came from Italy. Odds were all three were a bunch of out of work models or actresses who managed to get the accent down. It was all part of the game, and he loved it.

"So, ladies, can I get anyone a drink?" volunteered Robbie.

"Champagne," replied Milena, with the confidence of a woman who had been through the drill a million times. Her two companions nodded in agreement. "Yes, champagne would be nice."

Bethany glanced at her watch. "Well, I need to head over to McCarran. Some trust fund kid is flying in on his daddy's Gulfstream to celebrate his 21st with his friends." She chuckled. "God knows what they're gonna want." She turned and headed back in the direction of the casino floor. Without turning, she raised her hand above her head "TTFN, guys."

Jesse gave an abbreviated salute and was about to order a bottle of Cristal when the cell phone clipped to his belt went off. He looked at the caller ID.

"Yo, Nicky."

"Jesseee!" One word only and Jesse could tell that his friend was intoxicated. He was barely able to hear him with the loud music pounding in the background.

"Where are you guys? I can hardly hear you." He glanced at his watch as he spoke. *3:10 a.m.*

"Ghostbar, baby!" Screamed Nicky. "We have a private table outside on the patio. This place is packed with hot ass, Jess. You guys have to get up here!"

Jesse smiled at the three women standing in front of him. He held the phone tighter and placed his index finger in his other ear as if somehow that would block out the loud music on the other end of the phone. "Okay, Nicky, we'll be up in a few minutes. How's Joey-G making out?"

Nicky laughed. "It's been a good night. He hasn't knocked anyone out . . . yet."

Jesse hung up the phone and reattached it to the clip on his belt. He turned to face the group and grinned. "Okay, you guys ready to have some real fun?"

The Ghostbar was located high above the strip on the 55th floor of The Palms Hotel. The space-age lounge featured long rows of egg-shaped chairs that faced a wall of windows with views of the multi-colored lights that adorned Las Vegas Boulevard. Outside, an open-air sky deck offered panoramic views of the Strip and beyond, and the see-through acrylic deck allowed patrons to peer hundreds of feet below into the Skin Pool Lounge while they danced and drank until the sun came up.

The elevator doors opened, and Jesse walked into the lounge with Milena by his side. Robbie followed with his arm wrapped around Sofia's waist, and Luke and Giselle were so busy making out that they had yet to notice the elevator had stopped.

Needless to say, the group turned a few heads as they made their way through the chic, sultry lounge and headed out onto the sky deck. Once outside, Jesse took a breath of the cool early morning air. It was a welcome change from the stale, re-circulated, conditioned oxygen in the casino. There was a rock band playing and loud, heart-pounding music had the crowded dance floor moving rhythmically to the beat.

Jesse scanned the deck and spotted Nicky and Joey-G at a corner table set up against the acrylic glass on the edge of the rooftop. It seemed oddly dangerous. They were surrounded by four beautiful women and as many empty Cristal bottles. The entire corner was cordoned off by velvet rope, in front of which stood two burly bouncers.

"Hey, Jess, over here," called out Nicky.

"Hello, Mr. James," said one of the bouncers as he unclasped a section of the rope.

"'Sup, guys," said Jesse as he took a seat at the large round table.

Robbie, Luke and the three women all followed suit and Luke made the introductions.

Joey-G leaned into the table. "Place is kickin', huh, Jess?"

Jesse nodded his head and looked across the dance floor. It was packed with beautiful, half-naked women, bumping and grinding to the sounds of the *Californication* pumping through the band's speakers.

Nicky reached into his shirt pocket and took out a small pouch filled with white powder. He scooped out a small bump with the tip of his pinky, brought his finger to his nose and snorted back the coke. "My guy hooked us up," he said, offering the pouch to Jesse. "Got an eight-ball back at the room."

Jesse took a hit and then passed the bag to Milena. "Why don't you take the rest of the girls to the powder room?" he said, nodding in the direction of the entrance to the club.

Milena took the bag from Jesse and placed it in her purse. She placed her hands over his shoulders and brought her lips to his. She stood, smiled at him seductively and exited through the ropes with the rest of the women in tow.

Nicky looked across the table at Jesse, Robbie and Luke. His face had become serious. "Listen, guys, I don't want to be a buzz kill or nothin' but Joey and I were down at the sports book and we caught this news clip on one of the . . ."

"Hello, gentlemen," interrupted a dark-haired, middle-aged man, neatly dressed in a black suit with an open-collared shirt. Although he had a distinguished look about him, he seemed a bit out of place among the throngs that were less than half his age.

Jesse, Luke, Nicky and Robbie all looked over at the bouncers in amazement.

"What the fuck?" shouted Nicky, angrily.

Both bouncers shrugged their shoulders.

Joey-G stood to his feet and placed his hand on the man's shoulder. "Excuse me friend, but this is a private party," he said, tightening his grip.

The older man winced and then let out a slight chuckle. He turned up his palms in surrendering fashion. "Guys, I'm George Muldoon," he said extending his hand to Jesse.

"Who?"

"George Muldoon," he repeated, with question is his voice.

Still nothing.

"The Muldoon family?" said the man, this time with even more question in his voice.

Joey-G tightened his grip as the man cried out in pain.

"I own the place, I own the place," retorted the man quickly, agony in his voice. "My family owns and manages The Palms Hotel Casino and Resort . . ."

Joey-G's eyes narrowed for a moment then opened wide. Immediately, he let go of the man's shoulder. "Jeez, why didn't cha say so?" replied Joey, as he straightened out the man's jacket and gave him a pat on the back.

Jesse, Nicky, Robbie and Luke started cracking up hysterically. Then Jessie stood and stretched his hand over the table. "Nice to meet you, George. Sorry about the Picasso."

More laughter.

Muldoon was holding his shoulder where Joey-G had grabbed him. He let go momentarily, shook Jesse's hand, and then immediately brought his hand back to his shoulder. "Mr. James." Muldoon paused. He gestured to one of the chairs at the table. "May I?"

"Why not?" replied Jesse.

Muldoon took a seat. He signaled to a cocktail waitress who immediately brought over six glasses and a bottle of Macallan Scotch. She smiled at Jesse as she filled each of the glasses.

Muldoon picked up his glass, brought it to his nose and breathed in the aroma. "Macallan Fine Oak 30," he said proudly. He then began swirling his glass. "About 1000 bucks a bottle." He took a sip, smiled and set his glass back down on the table. "I took the liberty of having a case delivered to your sky villa, Mr. James."

Robbie shot back his drink in a single gulp. "What can we do for you, George?"

Muldoon frowned. "Well, gentlemen," he said, "The hotel would like to comp you for your stay here at The Palms." He then looked directly at Jesse. "Plus, we'd forgive any debt you may have incurred during your last visit."

Jesse grinned. "Why so gracious?"

"Yeah," echoed Luke. "Why so gracious, Jorge?"

Muldoon smiled. He reached for his glass, sat back in his chair and crossed his legs. "Well, boys, we were hoping Jesse would consider doing a few songs with the band," he said, nodding in the direction of the stage. "*Back Against the Wall,* and maybe two others from the new album."

Jesse looked over at his brothers. "What do ya think?"

"It's like 150 grand for three songs, Jess," replied Robbie.

"Yeah," interjected Luke. "I say go for it."

Jesse reached over and grabbed his glass of scotch. He sniffed it and swirled it around mockingly.

Robbie, Luke, Nicky and Joey-G all started cracking up again.

Jesse shot back the drink and began making a clicking noise with his tongue. "Yes, yes . . . quite nice, quite nice. I can really taste the woody flavor."

More laughter, harder now. Even Muldoon was smiling.

"Okay, Jorge, send up four more cases for my boys here and you got a deal."

CHAPTER 23

JAKE LAY AWAKE, staring at the ceiling in his room at the Beverly Hills Hotel. He glanced over at the alarm clock perched on a nightstand beside the bed and frowned. *5:15 a.m.* It seemed like he had been staring at that same spot on the ceiling for hours. He had arrived back at the room sometime after 2:00 a.m. and had reviewed the surveillance video Depass had burned for him so many times that the image of the killer's face was now imbedded in his brain. With sleep seemingly out of the question, Jake stood, made his way across the large room and stopped in front of the flat-panel plasma that was mounted to the wall. Other than the light from the television, the room was completely dark, as the sun had yet to rise. The picture was paused where Jake had left it earlier that morning, on a close-up of the killer's face as he exited the USC locker room. It was eerie and looked as if some deranged hotel employee had hung a sadistic portrait of a man's blood-covered face as a practical joke. Jake yawned. He then made his way to the bathroom, turned on the faucet full blast and leaned in, resting his elbows on the cool granite countertop. He looked at himself in the mirror and grimaced. "You look like shit," he said to his reflection. His eyes were dark with shadows and the lack of sleep was starting to show. He shook his head in disappointment. "Get it together, man," he mumbled, as he splashed cold water on his face and neck. He ran his wet fingers through his hair several times then shut off the faucet. He turned and grabbed an oversized towel, ran it over his face and hair, turned off the light and made his way back into the bedroom. Quickly, he threw on a pair of shorts, along with a T-shirt and running sneakers, grabbed his BlackBerry, and left the room for the hotel fitness center.

The room was dark and empty and why wouldn't it be? It was 5:30 on a Sunday morning, the sun had still not risen and any other sensible person at the hotel was fast asleep. Jake clicked on the lights and made his way past the rows of cardio equipment, through a set of sliding glass doors, and into a room that was used primarily for aerobics and kickboxing classes. There was a hardwood parquet floor, much like a basketball court, and the entire wall across from where he was standing was mirrored. In the corner of the room stood six black heavy bags, with the word Everlast across the center of each bag in large yellow letters. Jake pushed one of the bags to the center of the floor and grabbed a pair of medium weight sparring gloves from a plastic bin. The room was lit only by the thin streaks of light coming through the glass sliders from the adjoining room, and Jake found the darkness relaxing. He set his PDA down in front of the mirrored wall, slid on the gloves and approached the bag zealously.

After about 15 minutes, his hair was drenched with sweat and he was in perfect rhythm as he danced around the bag, striking it with great force. He felt strong, very strong, and he had great stamina for a man who hadn't slept in two days. He could hear the heavy plastic base clunk against the parquet floor as he jabbed and punched the big black bag, knocking it further back with every blow: right-right left, right-right left. "Keep your guard up!" he huffed, as he struck the Everlast so hard that it nearly toppled over on its sand-filled base. Jake smiled as he continued to spar with the bag and imagined it as the killer's face.

The image became more realistic with every blow and Jake began alternating the killer's face with that of Lefty Shapiro. He was just about to tackle the bag to the ground and beat it to a pulp when his BlackBerry went off, indicating a new e-mail. His chest was heaving and he gasped for air as he made his way across the wood floor. He hoped it would be from Krycerick with good news, but feared it would be from the killer taunting him with notice of another brutal homicide. Given his past experience with the LAPD, the latter seemed more probable.

Still breathing hard, Jake brought his right hand to his mouth, clenched the tip of the sparring glove between his teeth and pulled it off his fist. He spit it to the ground and then twisted off the other. With sweat dripping from his face, he knelt down in front of the phone and saw that the e-mail was from Jarvis.

Jake,

We ran that image you sent us from the USC locker room through the Bureau's face recognition data bank. The computer came back with a 99.9% identical match on all facial characteristics of a guy named Norris Burns. We cross-referenced the name with the license plate from the Ford Taurus and it's a match. He's our man!

But, Jake, here's where it really gets interesting. Norris Burns also goes by the name Burns Newman, and he's a card—carrying member of the Screen Actors Guild. I'll give you one guess who his agent is, or was, for that matter. You guessed it. Up until about a year ago, Norris Burns was represented by The Shapiro Talent Agency.

Once again, we're dealing with the wrath of a psychopath, huh, Jake?

"Or pride," muttered Jake, as he made his way across the empty room and grabbed a towel from a cabinet beside the sliding glass doors. He tossed it over his head and began to rub some of the sweat out of his hair. He dried his face and left the fitness center for his hotel room. On his way up, he considered calling Krycerick, but given the early hour, he thought an e-mail would be more appropriate. Although he wasn't sure if Lefty would be working on a Sunday morning, he stressed the need to get to the agency first thing. He then called Lefty, whom he didn't mind awakening at 5:30 a.m., but got voicemail at his home, office, and cell.

When he arrived back at the room, Jake immediately made his way to his desk, where the contents of Dr. Bonina's files were scattered about. He had reviewed her detailed notes and the gruesome photos from the two crime scenes several times earlier that morning, before focusing his attention on the surveillance tapes. He pulled open the desk drawer, took out a pen, and wrote the killer's name in capital letters across the top of one of the folders.

NORRIS BURNS AKA BURNS NEWMAN.

CHAPTER 24

JESSE JAMES STUMBLED THROUGH the sky villa on the 29th floor of the Palms Hotel, bleary eyed, clenching a half-empty bottle of Macallan Fine Oak 30 tightly in his fist. His shirt was unbuttoned, hanging loosely over his dark jeans, revealing his tan muscular chest and tight abs. His long black hair was pulled back in a tight ponytail and he wore a blue bandana over his head like a pirate. *Johnny Depp had nothing on him.*

"Why the fuck am I always the last man standing!" he shouted, his voice echoing off the walls of the cavernous, two-story, 9000 square foot suite. Loud, heart-pounding music was still blasting through the villa from the professional DJ booth that hung over the living room from a balcony on the second floor. Empty bottles of Cristal were littered throughout the room, and shards of broken glass were scattered about the floor beneath a tattered framed painting, the sight of which made Jessie chuckle. "I hope that's not another Picasso," he said, jokingly.

Everywhere he looked beautiful women were passed out, wearing little more than their bras and panties. Tattered hair, tanned skin and lots and lots of Victoria's Secret black lace. There must have been at least a dozen of them scattered about the couches and chairs throughout the enormous two-story living room. *It was good to be a rock star.*

His brothers Robbie and Luke had disappeared hours ago into one of the bedroom suites with the Italians. Nicky and Joey-G had made their way into the billiards parlor for a game of strip eight ball with a handful of models and hadn't been seen since.

Jesse gazed out onto the balcony. The sun was just starting to rise over the strip and the once-brilliant neon lights that adorned Las Vegas Boulevard seemed to suddenly lose their luster in the morning haze. Jesse made his way across the black marble floor and stepped out onto the balcony where more half-naked women were passed out on an assortment of multi-colored chaise lounges.

The large Egyptian stone balcony had an infinity edge swimming pool that jutted out several feet off the building, surrounded only by glass end walls. The crystal blue pool water was bubbling about with the first of the morning sun sparkling off its surface.

Jesse heard a grinding sound coming from the pool's filter and noticed something clogged in one of its skimmers. He made his way along one of the glass walls to the far end of the pool, reached down into the water and forced his hand deep into the skimmer. He pulled out a large pink bra with enormous D cups. He chuckled, eyed the undergarment appreciatively and then flung it to the side. He then turned to make his way back to the balcony when he realized where he was standing. "Why the fuck does everything have to be so close to the goddamn edge of the building," Jesse mumbled, recalling his table at Ghostbar. Cautiously, he peered over the side, looked down 29 stories, and shook his head. "I'm gonna have to have speak to Muldoon about this," he said, as he stepped away from the side

181

in the direction of a busty brunette who was peacefully sleeping on one of the lounges. Her face was covered in a mess of tangled, dark hair and she was wearing only a pair of thong panties. Jesse shook his head. "Fucking lightweights," he muttered, as he took a long tug on the bottle of scotch and then threw it against the wall, smashing it to pieces. The loud noise didn't seem to cause even the slightest stir in the sleeping woman. He gazed around the balcony. "Hey, any of you babes wanna party?" he shouted, and nearly lost his balance.

"I'll party with you, Jesse," came a voice from just beyond the large sliding glass doors that separated the balcony and the living room.

With a start, Jesse quickly turned in the direction the voice had come from, steadying himself by grasping one of the umbrella stands. He squinted his blood-shot eyes. "Who said that?" he asked, as he scanned the area through blurry vision.

Suddenly, a figure appeared through the open sliders and stepped out onto the balcony. "What's wrong, Jess? Cat got your tongue?"

It was Kimbra Reese, the young woman who had charged through the hotel lobby and dove into his arms earlier that morning. She was dressed in a black dress that clung to her body like it was painted on, and was holding an unopened bottle of Macallans. She tilted her head and held up the bottle. "Got any ice, rock star?"

Jesse grinned, then pointed to the woman. "Melanie, right?"

"Close enough."

Jesse steadied himself and walked across the Egyptian stone to the outdoor bar. He positioned himself behind the granite countertop and gestured to one of the barstools. "Have a seat," he said, as he filled two glasses with ice and set them down in front of him. His eyes narrowed. "How'd you get in here?" he asked.

Kimbra set the bottle down on the bar and fell back into one of the high back barstools. She retrieved a small magnetic key from her purse and slid it across to Jesse. "Your friend Nicky gave this to me this morning."

Jesse shook his head. "Nicky," he repeated, with a hint of laughter in his voice. He uncorked the bottle, filled both glasses and handed one to Kimbra. "Here ya go, beautiful," he said, and then guzzled down the drink in a single gulp. As he did, he glanced over Kimbra's shoulder at the brunette who made a groaning noise, shifted about and then settled back into her coma-like sleep.

Kimbra looked at the dark liquid curiously. "Oh well, bottoms up," she said, and then took a healthy sip. Her eyes widened as she began coughing and flapping her hand in front of her mouth in a waving motion. "Oh my God!" she exclaimed. "That's horrible."

Jesse smiled. "Yeah, you're supposed to swirl it around in your glass first."

"Blah!" She slid the glass across the bar to Jesse. "Not my thing," she said. She then nodded in the direction of a small mirror that lay flat on the corner of the bar. On it was several lines of coke and a tightly rolled 100-dollar bill. "But that is," she said with a naughty smile.

Jesse glanced over at the blow. "Be my guest," he said, as he slid the mirror in front of Kimbra.

She grinned as she brought both hands to the sides of her cheeks and combed her long blonde hair over her ears with her fingers. She reached for the rolled-up bill and brought it to her nose. She glanced over at Jesse, smiled, and uttered those four famous words: "What happens in Vegas . . ." She leaned over and filled each nostril with the white powder. "Oh baby!" she exclaimed, as she dropped the bill onto the mirror and fell back into her barstool.

Jesse laughed. "Good shit, huh?" He reached for the hundred, leaned in and snorted back a line.

Kimbra kicked off her shoes and leaned further back into her bar stool. She lifted one of her legs to the countertop and curled her toes around the edge of the granite. Slowly, she began rocking her leg back and forth revealing to Jesse that she wasn't wearing anything under her skirt. "So, rock star," she said, seductively. "Wanna fuck?"

Jesse nodded.

Kimbra then crawled up onto the bar directly in front of where Jesse was standing. She reached over and scooped up a small bump of coke onto her index finger and slid it into Jessie's mouth. Slowly, she extracted her finger and replaced it with her tongue as the two began to kiss passionately. Jesse lifted her from the bar and gently set her on the ground in front of him. Still kissing her, he slid the spaghetti straps from her shoulders and her dress fell to the ground. Kimbra leaned hard into Jesse, forcing his back against the wall. She began to kiss his neck, chest and stomach. Slowly, she sank to her knees as she unclasped his belt buckle and pulled his jeans and underwear to the floor. She smiled momentarily and then took him into her mouth.

Jesse let out a groan as he rested his head against the wall and closed his eyes, but when he reopened them, he saw something that he could not comprehend. It was the horrible sight of a man quickly approaching him with a long steel blade cocked high above his shoulder. "No!" Jesse screamed, as he brought his hand up to cover his face. The machete sliced through Jesse's wrist and neck with such force that it imbedded itself in the wall behind him.

Kimbra let out a horrific scream as Jesse's right hand and head both fell beside her. His body dropped to the floor with a thud and she was drenched in his blood as she looked up at the killer. "Oh my God, oh my God," she cried out repeatedly, trying to understand what had just happened. "What have you done?" she asked helplessly, her eyes filling with tears.

The Artist gave her a smile as he tugged hard on the handle and forced the machete from the wall. Blood was still dripping from its sharp blade as he slid it into his green duffel bag and extracted his signature small golden statue, which he placed on the bar beside the glass mirror. He made a clicking noise with his tongue and shook his head disapprovingly at Kimbra, who was now trembling with fear. "Don't you know this stuff'll kill ya?" he quipped, nodding at the coke. He then reached into her purse, took out her BlackBerry and held it in front of him. "Does this phone have a camera?"

Kimbra silently curled into a fetal position; she was covered in blood with a blank expression on her face. She was in shock.

"I said, does this have a camera!" he screamed.

The loudness of his voice startled her but her face remained expressionless. "Button . . . button . . . button . . . on the side," she said tearfully, as she began rocking back and forth on her bottom with her arms wrapped around her knees.

The Artist tilted the BlackBerry to the side. "Yes, so it does," he replied, as he knelt down beside her.

Kimbra gasped as she clenched her knees tighter to her chest and forced her body closer to the wall.

"There, there, little one. Nobody's gonna hurt you," he scowled. "You're not nearly famous enough." He leaned in close, held out the camera in front of them both, and snapped off a shot. He then stood and gazed down at the picture. "Lovely," he said, turning the screen to face her. "Although you look a little red in the face." He let out a sadistic laugh.

Kimbra didn't look up. She continued to rock, staring blankly into the distance.

The Artist shrugged. "Suit yourself," he said, as he attached the photo to a blank e-mail and sent the file to Jake. He then tossed the BlackBerry onto the bar and headed for the glass sliders. "See ya in the movies, baby!"

CHAPTER 25

JAKE LOWERED THE WINDOW to retrieve the small white parking voucher dangling about a foot-and-a-half away from his vehicle. As he tore the ticket from the automated security booth, its long wooden arm sprang to life, allowing him into the underground parking facility at the Century Towers Office Park. Jake floored it. The tires made a high-pitched screech as he sped down the narrow ramp, clenching the steering wheel so tightly that the veins in his forearms began to protrude.

"Easy, Jake," said Krycerick, from the passenger side seat. "We'll get this guy, I promise."

Jake clenched his teeth as he accelerated even faster through a series of sharp turns leading down to the lower levels of the garage. He jammed on the brakes, and the car came to a sudden halt in one of the parking spots. He pointed his finger at Krycerick and glanced down at his BlackBerry as he did so. The photograph The Artist had sent two hours earlier was displayed on the screen. "Look," he said, angrily. "This motherfucker is taunting me, and the longer it takes you guys to run down a simple plate, the more people this guy is gonna kill!"

Krycerick was silent. He knew Jake was right.

Jake grabbed the phone, got out of the car and headed for The Shapiro Agency. Krycerick followed and both men silently boarded the vacant elevator. Jake hit the button marked 44 and turned to face the Chief. "Nails, you've gotta understand. I haven't exactly had the best experience with the LAPD in the past." He glanced down at his BlackBerry for a moment and then held it up to Krycerick. "Now he's sending photos of himself." He paused. "It's like he wants to get caught."

Krycerick stared down at the photo. "Same blank expression as the video from USC." He squinted and concentrated harder on the small image. "Really not much to go on as far as location though. Maybe if we blow it up we'll see something."

Jake shook his head as he placed the phone inside his blazer pocket. "I have a feeling we'll be hearing from the woman in the photograph very soon."

Krycerick raised an eyebrow. "You don't think he killed her, Jake?"

"Doubt it," he replied. "Not unless she's connected to Shapiro somehow."

The doors to the elevator opened and the two men stepped out into the long hallway leading to the Shapiro Agency. Jake pushed open the glass doors and, as he entered the large waiting room, he was amazed at what he saw. Everywhere he looked angry people were demanding to speak with Lefty. It wasn't even 8:30 in the morning and already the entire place was packed with clients, publicists and lawyers, all concerned about the recent murders, all concerned about the Shapiro Slayer!

Tyler was seated at her desk, desperately trying to keep up with the barrage of incoming calls, all from clients expressing concern and fear. She looked frazzled as she toggled between blinking red lights with the eraser on her pencil. "Shapiro Agency, please hold . . .

Shapiro Agency please hold . . . No, sir, he's not in, but I will give him your message."

Just then Krycerick's cell went off. He flipped it open and looked down at the caller ID. "It's the department. Maybe they found something." he said hopefully, as he brought the phone to one of his ears and cupped the other with the palm of his hand. The busy room was growing noisier by the minute. He nodded at Jake and then in the direction of the glass doors. "Yeah, what do ya got?" he barked into the cell, as he headed back out into the hallway.

Jake turned and approached Tyler's desk. The smell of her perfume suddenly reminded him that Diane was flying in later that day and that he needed to be at LAX to meet her. Maybe Krycerick would have good news. Maybe LAPD tracked down that plate, found Norris Burns and right now he was in police custody swearing out a full confession. Somehow he doubted that.

"Good morning, Mr. Chase," said Tyler, forcing a slight smile. She unclasped her headset and placed it beside her phone that was now completely illuminated with every line flashing red. She frowned and stood. "He's on the golf course and he's not answering his cell. Is there anything I can help you with?"

She was dressed less professionally than the times he had seen her before. She was wearing a pair of jeans and a short-sleeved Polo. Her hair was pulled back and her face was devoid of all make-up. Nevertheless, she had a natural beauty that didn't seem to require much maintenance.

Jake turned the palms of his hands to the ceiling. "What's going on here?"

"Panic," replied Tyler. "Everyone's scared that they might be next." She nodded at a copy of *Variety* on her desk. The headline read SHAPIRO SLAYER CLAIMS ANOTHER VICTIM. "First that poor woman at Brooklyn Sims house, now Trevor Hash." She paused. "They seem to think the killer is after people from the agency."

The fax machine made a whirling sound and a small display panel on its front illuminated, displaying the words 'incoming fax.'

Tyler let out a sigh. "That's been going on all morning," she said as she walked behind her desk, retrieved the page from the machine and placed it on a stack of about a hundred just like it. She turned to face Jake. "Termination letters. All of them." She shook her head solemnly. "We lost half our clients this morning alone," she continued. She was silent for a moment and then said in a voice just above a whisper, "This is bad. This is really bad."

Jake retrieved his BlackBerry from his blazer and held the photo the killer had e-mailed him to Tyler. "Ms. Paige, do you recognize this man?"

Tyler let out a yelp. "Oh my God, is she dead?"

Jake glanced down at his PDA. The photo was rather gruesome, and he thought for a moment that he shouldn't have sprung it on her like that. He placed the phone back into his pocket and said, "No, we think she's fine, but the man in the photo is Norris Burns. He also goes by the name Burns Newman. We believe he is the killer and we also believe he is, or was, a client here."

Tyler repositioned herself in her chair. "I knew it," she said, as she wiggled a mouse around on a small blue pad, bringing her computer monitor to life. "I knew he was going to piss off the wrong guy sooner or later." Her phone was still ringing incessantly and the throngs of people gathered in the waiting room were multiplying and were beginning to grow impatient. Tyler ignored it all and typed the name Norris Burns on her keyboard. "Yup, here ya go," she said, pointing to the screen.

Jake leaned over her desk and read from the monitor. There wasn't much, just his name along with his stage name. There was also an address out in Pasadena, a phone number and a few headshots. Jake very much doubted that the address and cell were current, but wrote them down anyway. At the bottom of the profile were the words, CLIENT DIFFICULT—REPRESENTATION TERMINATED. It was dated July 2007.

Just then, Krycerick appeared shaking his head. He walked up to Jake and frowned.

"What now?" asked Jake.

"Nothin' yet on the plate. But I got good news and bad news on that room key." He paused. "The good news is that we tracked it to a motel on Sunset called *The Emperor's Crown.*"

"And the bad news," asked Jake.

"And the bad news is that around 1:00 a.m. someone torched the place. Burned it to the ground." Krycerick brought his hand to the back of his head. "Here's the weird part though. He checked into the motel using his real name. I mean why torch the place except to cover your tracks, right?"

"Wrong," replied Jake. "Charles Manson."

"What?"

"Charles Manson, Son of Sam, The Zodiac Killer, Mark David Chapman."

"Who?" asked Krycerick.

"The guy who killed John Lennon." Jake paused. "Look, it doesn't matter. The point is that they were all psychopaths and they all killed for the same reason. Attention. They want to be in the spotlight. They need to be in the spotlight. Fills some fucking void. Christ, he's probably sitting in front of a TV somewhere watching the news coverage of the fire with a fucking hard-on!" Jake took a deep breath and ran his fingers thorough his hair, thinking. He looked around the room and then back at Tyler. "Ms. Paige, you've got to get all of these people out of here. It's not safe. Not until we catch this bastard."

Tyler nodded. "Okay, Mr. Chase."

"Is there someplace where you can stay? Someplace other than your house?"

"Yes, I can stay with my sister for a while, I suppose."

"Good, do that," Jake replied as he leaned over and wrote a phone number on a small yellow pad on her desk. "I'm picking up my wife at the airport this evening. We will be at the house in Malibu around seven. This is the number if you need me."

Tyler looked down at the page and then back at Jake. "Why, Mr. Chase, do you think I am in any kind of danger?"

"Just get yourself to a safe place. I wouldn't take any chances with this guy." He then turned to Krycerick and grinned. "How's your golf game, Nails?"

CHAPTER 26

ANGLEBROOK GOLF CLUB WAS one of the most prominent and exclusive members-only golf courses in the country, if not the world. It was often compared to Augusta National and Torrey Pines, and this year's *Golf Digest Magazine* ranked it number one. Its membership read like a who's who of the wealthiest men and women from around the globe, including three past United States presidents, most of the Saudi royal family, a host of CEOs, business executives and captains of industry from major U.S. corporations, not to mention Tiger Woods. Located on the Palos Verdes Peninsula, the course sat high above the jagged California cliffs, offering its members over 7,300 yards of perfectly manicured fairways, lightning-fast, angulated greens and massive gleaming sand-white bunkers, all with stunning views of the Pacific Ocean and Catalina Island. However, before a person could even dream of setting his soft-spikes down on the 530 yard, par four, first hole, he had to first have been recommended by three existing Anglebrook members, undergone a full financial audit from the club's CPA, and withstood several tiers of scrutinizing interviews by board members, before being invited to pay the million dollar initiation fee.

Jake slammed on the brakes as his car fishtailed to a halt under the towering porte-cochere in front of the 40 thousand square-foot Anglebrook clubhouse. Sand and gravel flew everywhere as a huge cloud of dust billowed in the direction of two uniformed club attendants who appeared completely unamused. Jake jumped out of the car first, followed by Krycerick. He flung his keys over to one of the attendants and headed to the entrance. "Keep it close!"

"Excuse me, sir. You need to be a member to . . ."

"FBI!" replied Jake, as he held up his shield and continued into the building with Krycerick close behind.

"That works, too . . ."

Once inside the clubhouse, Jake and Krycerick were immediately approached by a tall handsome man casually dressed in tan kakis and a dark polo with the Anglebrook crest embroidered above its left breast pocket. *He had golf pro written all over him.* He gave Jake a curious look and extended a hand. "My name is Michael D'Angelo. I'm the club concierge." His gaze shifted between Jake and Krycerick. "Can I help you gentleman?"

Jake shook the man's hand and scanned the large, ornate room. The entrance where the three were gathered was completely covered in a tight-knit, hunter green carpet that extended well into the adjoining grillroom, where a large mahogany bar spanned the length of a mirrored wall. Attached to the mirror was a long mantel where an assortment of liquor bottles intermingled with a host of golf trophies, all bearing the Anglebrook logo on them. In front of the bar was a long row of high-back, leather bar stools, most of which were occupied by men who all looked strangely similar to D'Angelo with their khaki pants, polo shirts and golf caps. They all sipped from tumblers filled to the brim with Bloody Marys, complete with celery stalk, and their conversations all seemed to focus on their incredible golf scores, with the occasional gripe about the falling stock market.

"We need to have a look at your tee sheet," replied Jake. "It's imperative that we speak to one of your members immediately!"

D'Angelo looked concerned. "This is about Mr. Shapiro, isn't it?"

"Look, Mr. D'Angelo," interjected Krycerick. "We're in a bit of a rush."

"Of course," he replied. "Right this way," he said, making his way behind a glass-topped desk that was set off to the side of the grand entrance way.

Jake and Krycerick followed and watched as he began clicking away on his computer. Behind him stood a long row of large windows, and Jake noticed a group of men as they approached the first tee and began a series of stretching exercises. They were laughing among themselves and puffing away on expensive cigars as golf carts zoomed in every direction under the warm morning sun. Life appeared good at Anglebrook Golf Club.

"Here ya go, Mr. Shapiro and his group teed off at 6:30 this morning." He looked up at Jake and Krycerick. "Our golf carts all come equipped with GPS systems. Helps with distance to the pin."

"'Course they do," replied Krycerick.

D'Angelo looked back at his monitor. "They're on the 16th fairway." He then stood and nodded in the direction of a long hallway that led to the locker rooms and pro shop. "Our general manager, Matt Sullivan, will take you out to them."

As Sullivan sped Jake and Krycerick along the well-manicured, tree-lined 17th in one of the GPS equipped golf carts, Jake scrolled through a litany of e-mails that had been building up on his BlackBerry. The most recent was from Diane, who had sent a reminder that she was scheduled to land at LAX at 3:00 p.m. He glanced down at his watch. It was almost 9.

"So, Deputy Director," said Sullivan, breaking the silence. "Any interest in joining our little club? I mean, a man of your stature would fit . . ."

Suddenly, Jake's BlackBerry went off. He looked down at the caller ID. It was Jarvis. "Excuse me for a moment, Mr. Sullivan," he said, as he placed the phone over his ear. "Yeah, Jarvis. Whatcha got?"

"It's not good, Jake."

Jake sighed as the cart cruised past the 17th tee box in the direction of the 16th green. He uttered a single word. "Who?"

"That rock star, Jesse James." He paused. "Decapitated just like the others."

"And the gold statue?"

"Yeah, same signature. Small plastic Academy Award. Shapiro Talent Agency on the plaque."

"How 'bout the girl?" asked Jake.

"Her name is Kimbra Reese. Some groupie who was in the wrong place at the wrong time. She's fine, as far as . . . well, ya know." He hesitated for a moment. "Anyway, they were in Vegas at the Palms Hotel. That photo you sent me was taken at one of the sky villas there."

Jake covered the phone with his hand and leaned back to Krycerick. "We found the latest victim. Jesse James . . . at one of the hotels in Vegas."

Krycerick shook his head and clenched his fists.

"Okay, I'm on my way," replied Jake.

"Yeah, here's the thing, boss. The owner of the hotel heard you were working the case out in LA. Said he's heard of you by reputation." Jarvis paused. "Paramount . . . anyway, he's sending a chopper for you now."

"Fine," replied Jake. "And Brooklyn Sims?"

"She used her American Express card to check into some chi-chi spa out in Palm Springs, but when our field guys got there this morning, she had already gone. Seems like she's on the run, Jake. No worries though, we'll have her soon." There was a long pause. "Oh, and boss," continued Jarvis. "We triangulated your cell for the chopper pilot." A longer pause. "Um, are you playing golf?"

"Not exactly," replied Jake, as he hung up the phone and looked off into the distance. He could see a group of four men all-trudging along the fairway in the direction of their respective golf balls. They were all wearing what appeared to be the Anglebrook uniform, khaki pants, polo shirt, golf cap and, of course, the expensive stogie.

Krycerick noticed it as well and gave Sullivan a nod from the back of the cart. "You fellas have a secret handshake here too?"

Sullivan laughed as he pulled the cart up beside Lefty. "Good morning, Mr. Shapiro," he said. "You have some visitors."

Jake and Krycerick jumped off the golf cart and approached Lefty.

"Deputy Director," said Lefty smugly. "I had no idea you were a player." Then he laughed and glanced over at his three companions. "Gentlemen, I'd like you to meet FBI Deputy Director Jake Chase."

The three men gave a brief wave as they continued to study the positioning of their golf balls.

Jake nodded in Krycerick's direction. "This is LAPD Chief Eddie Krycerick."

Lefty raised an eyebrow. "Nails Krycerick?" he replied, shaking his head approvingly. "Your reputation precedes you, Chief." He then turned back to Jake. "Obviously you guys aren't here to play eighteen."

"No, we're not," replied Jake. His voice was more deliberate now. "There have been two more homicides." He reached into his blazer pocket and took out the morning edition of Variety Tyler had given him. "I suppose you haven't seen this yet," he said, handing it over to Lefty.

Lefty took the paper from Jake and read the headlines. It was disturbing to say the least. SHAPIRO SLAYER CLAIMS ANOTHER VICTIM. He saw the picture of Trevor Hash and suddenly his face turned pale with anguish. He struggled to regain composure as he handed the magazine back to Jake. "Listen, k . . ." He was about to refer to Jake as kid, but remembered what Jake had told him about shooting him in the leg back at the office and thought better of it. He took a deep breath. "Jake, this doesn't mean anything." His voice was shaky. "It's just a coincidence."

"And the statue the killer leaves with your name on it," interjected Krycerick. "That a coincidence too?"

Lefty appeared dumbfounded. For once, he was speechless.

Jake shook his head. He noticed that Lefty's cigar-smoking buddies had stopped what they were doing and all eyes were now on him and Krycerick. "Unfortunately, it doesn't end there. There was another murder early this morning." He paused. "Another client of yours."

Lefty stared blankly at the ground. He braced himself. "Who?" he asked solemnly.

"Jesse James."

Lefty closed his eyes. "Another gold statue?"

"I'm afraid so," replied Jake. "We're pretty sure the killer used to be a client of yours. Burns Newman."

Jake waited for a reaction but none came.

"Mr. Shapiro," said Krycerick. "I think we need to get you into protective custody. At least until we catch this guy."

"What for?" replied Lefty. "I'm already dead in this town."

Just then the thumping of chopper blades whipping through the calm morning breeze startled the group. It came soaring in over the tree line and landed in the middle of the 16th fairway as khaki pants and polo shirts everywhere ran for cover. *Someone yell fore!*

"What the fuck's that?" asked one of Lefty's cronies in a startled voice.

"My ride," replied Jake, over the noise from the chopper. He looked at Krycerick. His hair was blowing in the wind. "Make sure he comes with you," he shouted, pointing to Lefty. "He's not safe out here." He ducked his head and ran in the direction of the chopper. He looked back at Krycerick and called out over the loud noise coming from the propellers. "And another thing, get Dr. Bonina and her team to the Palms Hotel—ASAP!"

CHAPTER 27

THE ARTIST COULDN'T HAVE BEEN more pleased with himself. Aside from the Brooke Sims snafu, which he intended to rectify shortly, the weekend was going exactly as planned. And what a weekend it was! He was now officially famous—or was it infamous? It didn't matter; either way, the entire country now knew the name Burns Newman, perhaps the entire world. He wanted to roll down the widow and scream his name at the top of his lungs, but he fought hard to control the temptation. After all, he didn't want to get caught, at least not yet. It wasn't time. Instead, he drove the Chrysler LeBaron she had rented for him well within the speed limit as he surfed through the radio stations, stopping on any one that was discussing the horrific murders.

As planned, he would be back in LA by noon and if all went well, by 12:01 p.m. Jake Chase would be dead. He cringed at the thought that he wouldn't be able to use his machete to cut off Jake's head like all the others; that was not the way she wanted it. It had to be a magnificent explosion. It had to be an eye-popping, earth-shattering blast that would rattle the living room as people watched in hi-def, Dolby digital surround sound on 60-inch plasma TVs. And the Paramount case that had made Jake famous would provide the perfect ironic twist for this blockbuster. That was Hollywood!

The Artist looked at the passenger side seat and spied his cell phone. He wanted so much to call her but knew it was completely against the rules. He knew that even the slightest deviation from the plan would send her into a fit, and he already had one strike against him after failing to kill Brooke. He took a deep breath and exhaled slowly. *Fuck it.* He didn't care about the rules anymore. He was on top of the world and he wanted to share it with someone, and for now, she was the only one. With one hand on the steering wheel, he picked up the phone and dialed her number. It was a number he had dialed so many times in the past that it was now permanently imbedded into his memory. After two rings she picked up.

"Are you fucking crazy!" she whispered through the receiver. "Why are you calling me at work?"

"I just wanted to tell you that I love you and that, well um, that I have never been happier."

There was a long silence—so long that The Artist looked down at his phone to make sure that the call had not been dropped. Then she spoke, still whispering. "I love you, too." More silence. "Did you set the device?"

The Artist nodded as he changed lanes and raced past a slow-moving 18-wheeler. "Yes, exactly like we planned. Just enough C4 plastique to take out the room." He looked in the rear view mirror and watched as the large truck faded into the distance. "It won't be another World Trade Center. I set it to go off at noon." He gazed at the clock on the dashboard. *11:05.* "Do you think that's enough time for him to get there?"

"Yes, I am sure of it," she replied confidently. "Now I have to hang up. I will see you tonight at the Skyline Motel." Then she was gone.

CHAPTER 28

JAKE LOOKED OUT THE WINDOW of the twin-prop Bell JetRanger III as it cruised at low altitude east over the Mojave Desert in the direction of Las Vegas. It was not a very picturesque flight, just dry sand and tumbleweeds, broken up only by the occasional pack of wild coyotes chasing down some helpless animal or the lone mountain lion slumbering peacefully on a ridge in the hot desert sun. The large black headsets worn by both Jake and the chopper pilot muffled the loud whipping sounds coming from the twin propellers. Just then, Jake noticed a large body of water that looked completely out of place in the otherwise arid reserve. He pointed to the water as he angled the tiny mouthpiece connected to the headset closer to his lips. Even though his voice was being transmitted into the pilot's earphones electronically, he still had to shout. "Looks like a mirage."

The pilot chuckled. "Yeah, Lake Mead," he replied. "It's the largest reservoir in the U.S." He then angled the aircraft so that Jake could have a better look. "Created with the construction of the Hoover Dam." Then he pointed off into the hazy distance at the multitude of hotels and high-rise buildings that make up the brief Las Vegas Skyline. "Las Vegas strip," he shouted. "We'll be landing soon."

As the chopper gently touched down on the rooftop helipad at the Palms Hotel, Jake undid his safety harness, hung his headset on a hook beside the windshield and was about to exit the aircraft when the pilot grabbed him by the shoulder. "Look son, name's Chuck, Chuck Parker," he said, as he slid his headset around the back of his neck and adjusted his aviator sunglasses. "I've been reading a lot about you. If you need anything—I mean anything." He handed over a business card. On its front was the image of a military helicopter along with his name and phone number. "I flew three tours in Korea." He paused. "Heard your pop was in Korea." Another pause, this time longer. "Probably a good man," he continued, nodding his head.

Jake took the card and stared down at it for a moment before placing it into his pocket. "He was, Chuck. He was a very good man." He then extended his hand. "Thanks for the lift," he said with a grin. "And I may just take you up on your offer," he continued as he jumped down onto the helipad, ducked his head and ran to the entrance of the building.

"Good morning, Deputy Director. My Name is George Muldoon, I own the hotel."

Some people are forced to fly coach and fight the baggage terminal for hours before dragging their luggage to the long lines at the overcrowded check-in counter in the hotel's lobby, while others have the privilege of strolling through the hotel carelessly, in the direction of the VIP check-in lounge, where they're served cocktails by beautiful half-naked women . . . and then there's Jake Chase.

Of course, being flown to the rooftop of the hottest hotel in Vegas by an ex-marine chopper pilot in the hotel's private helicopter, and being greeted on the roof by none other than the owner of the hotel himself, wasn't Jake's style at all. It never was, and it never would be. But he had a job to do and he had to get it done soon!

Was it actually morning? Jake glanced down at his watch. *It was.* "Good morning, Mr. Muldoon," he replied, as the two men shook hands. "Can you take me to the crime scene?"

"Of course," replied Muldoon. "Right this way." He led Jake into the building and onto a private elevator. "The villa is located on the 29th floor. "Las Vegas Forensics has been here for about an hour."

"And the girl?"

Muldoon shook his head. "Poor thing. An ambulance took her to Las Vegas General about 15 minutes ago. She's not harmed, but she's still in complete shock."

The elevator chimed and the doors opened on the 29th floor. Muldoon gestured for Jake to proceed. "One of Mr. James' brothers found her curled up in the fetal position next to Jesse around 9:30 this morning. We immediately called LVPD and then we called you."

"Okay, Mr. Muldoon. I'm gonna need you to run interference with the media. I'm sure they're circling your building like vultures."

Muldoon nodded.

The two men stopped in front of a large oak door with the words SKY VILLA II spelled out in gold letters across its front. A uniformed LVPD officer was standing guard.

"Detective, this is FBI Deputy Director Chase. Please see to it that he is given everything he needs."

"Of course, Mr. Muldoon."

"Detective," said Jake, "I want an immediate evacuation of floors 24 through 34. Five above and five below. And try to do it without causing too much of a panic."

The police officer looked at Muldoon who just shrugged his shoulders.

"Do as he says, Detective."

"And another thing," said Jake, now addressing both men. "The bureau has several photos of the suspected killer. They have been e-mailed to the LVPD department chiefs as well as to the head of your in-house security team, Mr. Muldoon. I want that photo quickly circulated and I want every man and woman from both agencies looking for this guy. Got it?"

"Got it, Jake."

Jake then turned to face Muldoon who appeared to be hanging on his every word. "When Dr. Bonina and her team arrive, make sure they are extended every possible courtesy."

"Of course," replied Muldoon. "I'll show them up myself." He took a deep breath as a look of concern came across his face. "Is there anything else, Deputy Director?"

"That's it for now," replied Jake, as he pushed open the door and entered the Sky Villa. "I'll catch up with you later."

The large two-story suite was packed with people scattered about and appeared far less organized than LA. Las Vegas police and forensics personnel were matched in force with hotel security as everyone trampled the crime scene without the slightest bit of concern for the preservation of evidence. Close to 30 people in all, there appeared to be an ongoing power struggle between the three agencies and, although he hated to admit it, Jake actually missed being in Los Angeles with Krycerick and

Bonina. He held up his credentials and grabbed a young forensic examiner by the shoulder. "Who's in charge here?"

The examiner nodded in the direction of the pool. "Gaynor," he said. "Captain Paul Gaynor."

"Thanks," replied Jake.

He then made his way across the shiny, black marble floor, through the sliders, and out onto the lanai. Although Jesse's body had already been taken to the coroner's lab, the blood-drenched Egyptian stone floor, walls and ceiling painted an eerie picture of the horrific death that had been bestowed upon him several hours before.

Behind the bar was a large pool of blood where Jesse was initially struck. It streamed off in various directions creating smaller reservoirs at various locations around the grand lanai. Jake noticed several sets of bare footprints in the drying blood, all heading from a group of lounge chairs beside the swimming pool that proceeded through the villa in the direction of the front door. He wondered why he hadn't noticed them when he initially entered the villa, and, more importantly, why everyone was now trampling all over them. "In-fucking-credible," he murmured to himself.

Carefully, he made his way to the bar that was also coated in dried blood. Once again he held up his identification. "Captain?" he asked, as he continued to survey the area.

"Yeah, who's askin'?" replied Gaynor. Then he squinted and read Jake's ID. Suddenly his eyes opened wide. "Holy shit, it's you!"

Jake sighed. "Look Captain, we're going to need to get all these people out of here," he said, motioning in the direction of the villa. "This crime scene is being completely compromised, and I have my own people on their way."

Gaynor placed his hand on the back of his neck and began shaking his head from side to side. "Yeah, see, I'm not so sure that anyone . . ."

Just then, something under one of the barstools caught Jake's eye. It was nothing more than a brief flicker of red light reflecting off what seemed to be the only blood-free section of Egyptian stone left on the entire lanai. He held up his hand to Gaynor and stared down at the floor waiting to see if somehow he had imagined it. But there it was again: a second time, then a third, and then a forth. It was coming from under the bar. He knelt down on one knee, gently slid back one of the barstools, and arched his body under the ledge.

Gaynor gave him a sideways look. "What are you doing?" he asked curiously.

Jake didn't answer. Instead, he reached up into the seam under the bar and carefully retrieved a small rectangular box. It was about the size of a standard masonry brick and inside its aluminum casing was enough C4 plastique to take out most of the hotel's 29th floor. Slowly, Jake rose to his feet. Gently, he turned the device so that a small LCD screen faced him. It continued to flash red digital numbers as it counted down the minutes and seconds to detonation. 2:46 . . . 2:45 . . . 2:44 . . .

Gaynor took a step back. "Is that what I think it is?"

"Well," replied Jake. "If you think it's a bomb, then yes, Captain, it's exactly what you think it is." Jake looked back down at the LCD screen, considering his options. 2:36 . . . 2:35 . . . 2:34. He could feel his pulse begin to race as his brain searched for the right move. Dropping it over the ledge would certainly save everyone in the sky villa but who knows how many innocent bystanders on the street would be killed? *Think, think, think.*

Quickly, he made his way back through the glass sliders and into the suite. "Okay, people, listen up!" he shouted.

Suddenly, everyone stopped what they were doing and all eyes were now on him.

"My name is Jake Chase. I am the Deputy Director of the Federal Bureau of Investigations." The once boisterous room had now become so quiet you could hear a pin drop. "I need to know if anyone here has any training in defusing a bomb."

The news sent a flurry of chatter about the room.

"People," shouted Jake, "there isn't much time." Military training. Has anyone here had any military training in explosives?"

No response.

Jake looked at the device. Time was quickly running out. He had less than two minutes until detonation. He thought about calling Eddie Maloney, one of the bomb techs back at Quantico. He was certain that Eddie could talk him through defusing just about any bomb there was, but there just wasn't enough time. He took one last look down at the counter, which now read *1:04* and then began screaming at the top of his lungs. "Get out! Get the fuck out! Everyone out now! Move, move, move . . ."

He sounded like a raving lunatic, but it worked. It was a mass exodus. Like a heard of stampeding bulls all heading for the door at once, the room began to empty.

"Jake, what the fuck are you doing?" asked Gaynor. "It's suicide man."

Jake pointed to the door. "Get your men as far away as possible," he screamed. He then looked down at the device. "I'm pretty sure this is C4. I've dealt with this stuff before. If I can get it far enough away from the building, I think we'll all be a safe distance from the blast!"

"Far enough away from the building!" Gaynor shouted in exasperation. "How the fuck are you gonna do that?"

"Captain, leave that to me. Now, get the fuck out of here!"

Gaynor began walking backwards in the direction of the front door. He raised the palms of his hands to Jake. "Sorry, man. I have a wife and a little boy." He then turned and darted out the door, leaving Jake alone with the bomb.

Without wasting a second, Jake headed back through the sliders and onto the lanai. He set the bomb down on the countertop and glanced down at the LCD panel. *0.57 . . . 0.56 . . . 0.55 . . . . He* then walked behind the bar and retrieved Jack Daniels and a small shot glass. He set the glass down and filled it to the rim. He held up the glass and tilted it in the direction of the bomb in a mock salute. 0.34 . . . 0.33 . . . 0.32 . . . . He knew he only needed seven seconds to launch the bomb off the building and, he hoped, get it a safe distance away before it went off. Any more than seven seconds and he ran the risk of it falling to the street and killing innocent people; any less, and it would not be a safe distance from him. So seven seconds it was. He took a deep breath, shot back the whiskey, and grabbed the device like a football. His heart was racing so hard it felt like it was going to beat right out of his chest. "Jake, what the fuck are you doing!" he screamed, as he positioned himself several feet in front of the pool. 0.12 . . . 0.11 . . . 0.10 . . . Suddenly, he charged full speed ahead toward the water, and when he reached the edge, he cocked his arm and launched the device into the air with as much force as his body could muster. He nearly toppled over the coping and into the water but managed to catch his balance as he watched the bomb sail over the glass rail and soar high into the sky. "Yeah!" he screamed, as the device climbed higher and higher and further and further away from the building. *Tick . . . tick . . . tick . . . boom!* Suddenly, there was a flash of light followed by an explosion so loud his ears instantly filled with pain—a pain that was quickly replaced by a loud ringing and shockwaves that sent him into the air, crashing through the glass sliders. He flew across the sky villa, crashed head first into one of the stone pillars and then fell lifelessly to the black marble floor.

CHAPTER 29

JAKE SLOWLY OPENED HIS EYES and struggled hard to focus both his vision and thoughts, trying to determine where he was and how he got there. His entire body ached and he could feel a myriad of small tubes connected to one of his arms, the other bound close to his chest by a cloth sling. The room was dark with the shades drawn and Jake could see hospital activity through the glass pane on his door, although no one had yet noticed he was awake. His mouth was parched and his head pounded as he struggled to sit upright in his bed. A jolt of pain from his head sent shockwaves throughout his entire body, and he grimaced as he fell back down onto his pillow. "Not good," he muttered to himself as he tried to sit up again, this time much slower. Carefully, he removed his arm from the sling; it didn't appear to be broken. He brought his hand to the side of his face and he could feel swelling around his right eye and a tightly woven row of stitches along his brow. He chuckled. "Diane's gonna love this one," he said as he tossed off the cover and put his feet to the floor. "Diane!" he shouted as he quickly looked up at the clock mounted to the wall. *5:10*. He had been out all afternoon.

Just then the door to his room burst open as two nurses came running to the side of his bed. "Please, Mr. Chase," said one of the nurses as she placed her hand gently on his shoulder, "you have to lay back down. You have a very serious concussion." She then signaled for the other nurse to elevate the back of the bed.

Jake squinted at a small silver name badge pinned to the nurse's uniform: Alicia Leo. "Ms. Leo, I don't think you understand. I'm with the FBI and I need . . ."

"I know who you are, Deputy Director," interrupted the nurse. She seemed sympathetic yet stern, all the while very professional. Carefully, she guided his arm back into the sling. "Chief Krycerick and Director Robbins were here all afternoon."

"Here? Robbins was here?" Jake asked, with a hint of concern in his voice.

"Yes," she replied. "They both were. In fact, they just left about a half hour ago," she continued, as she reached into her pocket and pulled out a piece of hospital stationery that was folded in half. "And I have strict orders from Mr. Robbins himself to keep you here until the doctor feels that you are well enough to leave."

Jake shook his head and once again removed his hand from the sling. Then he grinned and stood to his feet. "Trust me, honey, I've been through a lot worse than this," he said, as he gazed around the room for his clothes and personal effects.

Ms. Leo handed over the stationery and smiled. "He said you'd say that."

Jake gave her a quizzical look and took the note. He opened and began to read. It was a letter from the director.

Jake,

Unfortunately, I am needed back at Quantico. I have consulted with the medical staff and they all assured me you would be fine, but absolutely need to rest. A mild concussion, some powder burns and a sprained arm. Quite amazing, considering, but this isn't the first time your hard head has saved you.

Chief Krycerick is confident that LAPD will have the killer apprehended by morning and I assured him that he has my full support.

So get some sleep and let us throw a few relief innings for a change.

Martin Robbins.

Jake crumpled up the letter and dropped it to the floor. "Fuck that, I'm outta here!"

Leo smiled. "He said you'd say that too." She then nodded at the other woman. "Nurse, if you wouldn't mind."

"Certainly," she replied, as she turned a small valve on one of the machines that was connected to the tubes leading to Jake's arm. Suddenly, a clear fluid began quickly flowing through the tube and into his vein.

"Just a little something to help you rest . . . honey," said Leo, with a cocky smile.

Jake looked back and forth between the two women. "You don't understand. I need to . . ."

Jake's eyes rolled into the back of his head and he was out.

At 2:00 a.m. the sound of his hospital room door squeaking loudly and then banging shut awoke Jake with a start. The room was much darker now, and the busy hospital activity had settled down to one or two nurses on the night shift. He was disoriented from the drugs, but the pain in his head and arm had subsided. Slowly, he sat up and looked around the dark, empty room. He needed to get to a phone and call Diane to let her know that he was all right, and he needed to speak to Krycerick for an update. He tossed the sheets aside and swung his feet to the floor. He was about to stand when he heard the noise again. Someone was in the room with him. He squinted against the darkness and could make out the silhouette of a person approaching him. His mind raced. The drugs had not completely worn off and he fought hard to concentrate. If it was Leo or one of the doctors, they would have turned on the light or at least identified themselves by now. Quickly, he scanned the large room and spotted his clothes hanging in a closet at the other end of the room. Perhaps his gun and shoulder holster were there as well. Without wasting a second, Jake tore the IVs from his wrist and dove across the room sliding to position in front of the closet door. Still on the floor Jake reached in and pulled out his Glock 9. He rolled over onto his belly and pointed it in the direction of the intruder. "Freeze, scumbag!"

The shadow stopped moving forward. Instead, the person slowly knelt down and brought her face into a small ray of moonlight that was peeking through a seam in the curtains. "Is that a Glock you're holding, or are you just happy to see me, Deputy Director?" asked Brooklyn Sims, sarcastically.

Jake's eyes widened in disbelief as he realized that he almost shot the woman he was supposed to be protecting right between the eyes. He sighed in exasperation as he quickly engaged the safety catch on the Glock, pointed the gun at the ceiling and dropped his head onto his forearms. "I fucking hate LA," he muttered into the floor.

After a moment's reflection, Jake looked up at Brooke. "What are you doing here? We have FBI agents looking all over LA for you," he said as he stood and swung open the closet door. He stepped into his pants, drew them to his waist and then pulled the hospital gown over his head. "You are in great danger."

Brooke nodded. "I know I am," she replied. Her voice sounded more concerned now. "Can you help me?"

Jake buttoned his shirt and slid his shoulder holster around each arm. He threw on his blazer and combed his hair off his face with his fingers. He nodded. "Yes, but you have to do what I say," he replied, glancing out the window at the hospital parking lot.

"I will," replied Brooke. She paused and began biting her lower lip. "I just don't want to end up like . . ." her voice trailed off.

Jake noticed her look of concern. "No one else is gonna die!" he replied. His voice was deliberate and reassuring. "Now, where are you parked?"

Brooke didn't answer. She still appeared troubled and deep in her own thoughts.

Jake placed his hand on her shoulder. "Don't worry, this guy is not going to harm you, I promise you that."

"How can you be so sure?"

"'Cause now I'm pissed!" he replied, as he traced his fingers along the small line of stitches above his eye. "Now let's get the fuck out of here."

As the two made their way across the dark parking lot, Brooke reached into her purse and took out a small key ring. She pushed in on a plastic button with her thumb and a chirping sound came from the hood of a bright red Lamborghini Gallardo that was parked beside a lamppost.

As he reached for the key ring Jake's eyes widened. He smiled. "I'll drive."

CHAPTER 30

THE ARTIST LAY NAKED, STARING at the ceiling from his disheveled bed in the small room he had rented at the Skyline Motel. It was dark, with the only light coming from the flickering neon sign at the hotel's entrance just off Sunset. The pillows were scattered about, some on the bed, some on the floor, and the sheets were in complete disarray from the marathon sex they had just had. He glanced in the direction of the clock radio. *5:15 a.m.* He was still covered with their perspiration; he could smell her scent on his body, and it made him smile. Her wonderful smell hung in the room and attached itself to him, giving him reason to believe that she was actually there and not just a figment of his imagination. He turned on his side to face her side of the bed, but she was gone.

The Artist closed his eyes and hoped when he re-opened them she would be lying there smiling at him—perhaps running her fingers through his hair and telling him how much she loved him. But when he opened his eyes again there was still a void where she once was, if indeed, she was ever there at all. He sighed and swung his feet to the floor. He cradled his face with his hands and then ran his fingers through his hair. He was confused. He needed the pills.

Slowly, he reached over and grabbed a pack of cigarettes from the nightstand. For a long moment he stared at the cardboard package desperately trying to get a grasp on what was real and what was not. He gazed around the room as the red neon light intermittently flashed, briefly illuminating the walls in a fluorescent red hue and then leaving him in complete darkness. He lit the cigarette, stood and made his way in the direction of his green duffel. It was on the floor by the front door where he had left it the night before, and it contained, among other things, his pills—and right now he felt like he needed the whole bottle. He took a long drag and was just about to reach for the shoulder strap when he heard a noise. It was coming from the bathroom. Quickly, he turned and noticed a dim light peeking out under the bottom of the door. He stood motionless, confused. Then he heard the sound of the toilet flushing and water running from the faucet. The light disappeared and the door slowly opened.

Tyler exited the bathroom and made her way across the room to where he was standing. Her hair was tousled and her lithe, naked body was covered in sweat. She grinned wickedly, and with the red neon light reflecting off her glistening body, she looked evil. She reached for the cigarette and took a long drag. "What's wrong, Burnsie; you're not losing your nerve on me are ya?" Then she laughed and handed him back the cigarette.

"No, 'course not," he replied, still somewhat shaken. "But I just don't know how we're gonna find Brooklyn Sims." He paused and watched as Tyler slid into a tight pair of jeans. "I mean, if she's not at Palm Canyons anymore, she could be anywhere."

Tyler reached over to retrieve her bra and shirt from her overnight bag and then reconsidered. Instead, she stood up and made her way back to where The Artist was standing. Seductively, she wrapped her arms around his shoulders and pressed her body tightly against his. She brought her mouth inches from his ear. "We don't need that bitch anymore," she whispered. "Because of the Shapiro Slayer, Lefty has no more clients. He is done . . . finished." She then kissed him softly on the lips. "Don't forget what he did to you, baby," she said, still whispering, her mouth close to his. "You were going to be somebody in this town. A superstar. And then he ended that with a single phone call."

Tyler looked in his eyes and she knew she had him entranced in her spell. *What a fool*, she thought. She then pulled him even closer, pressing her bare breasts against his chest. "You'll never work again in this town. Remember that?"

The Artist nodded.

"Well, because of you, Marty Shapiro will never work again in this town." She kissed him again, this time playfully biting his bottom lip between her teeth. "And trust me," she continued. "To that fat pig, that is a fate worse than death!"

The Artist smiled. He then began kissing her, harder and more passionately than she ever had. He reached down and undid the button on her jeans.

Tyler took a step back and quickly brought her hands to his. "No!" she protested, and then forced a smile. "Not now, baby," she said, in a less abrasive tone, as she redid the button on her jeans and made her way back to her overnight bag. "You've gotten what you want, now it's my turn," she said, as she slipped her arms into the straps on her bra and connected the plastic clasp under her breasts. Leaning in over the credenza, she pulled her hair back and stared closely at her reflection in the mirror. "Jake Chase is still alive. For this to work, he must be killed."

The Artist shook his head. "That's not going to be easy." He paused. "I mean, that guy is like . . ."

"I don't want to hear it," interrupted Tyler adamantly. She then reached into her jeans pocket, took out the note Jake had given her and handed it to The Artist. "The derring-do FBI agent is staying at his beach house in Malibu with his precious little wife." Tyler let out a sarcastic laugh. "Feel free to kill that bitch too. It'll make for a better ending, anyway."

The Artist looked down at the address and then back at Tyler. "And then I'll see you in six months?"

Tyler pulled her polo over her head drew closed the zipper on her bag and threw the strap over her shoulder. She approached The Artist and gave him a final hug. "Yes, once Jake is dead, you turn yourself in to Chief Krycerick. I wrote his number down on the back of the note card."

The Artist glanced back down at the card and nodded. "It will all be done today, I promise."

"And you don't speak to anyone except Dave Kossow," continued Tyler. "He is the best lawyer money can buy." *And not a bad fuck either.* She handed over a second business card. *Davis Kossow, Esq.* "Then I will come and see you. Six months should be enough time for the media frenzy to have simmered down a bit."

The Artist stayed silent and paid close attention to what she was saying. He didn't want to screw this up now. He wanted to do this for her.

"Dave will draw up all of the papers. All you have to do is sign and leave the rest up to me." She grinned. "I promise I will make you more famous than you could ever imagine."

The Artist smiled. He was finally going to be in the movies. *Well, sort of.*

Tyler pulled open the door to the motel room and stepped outside. It was still dark and the morning air was cool. She knew from Lefty that the Jake Chase movie rights would fetch over 100 million in the open market, but she also knew that would never happen. Not even if she did manage to seduce Jake Chase. However, the rights to the killer's story in the death of the famous FBI agent would probably cash in close to a half a billion and that was something well within her control. It was indeed the most perfectly orchestrated Hollywood movie deal in the history of Hollywood movie deals.

CHAPTER 31

THE SUN WAS JUST BEGINNING to rise over the jagged Malibu bluffs as Jake raced the Lamborghini Gallardo along the Pacific Coast Highway in the direction of his home in the exclusive Point Dume section of Malibu. He could see the morning rays of sunlight glistening off the ocean's surface as he cruised the race car along the picturesque highway at 100 miles an hour. His arm was beginning to throb, and he wished he hadn't abandoned the sling back at the hospital as any sudden movement caused excruciating pain in his neck and shoulder.

Brooke, who had dozed off hours ago, was now peacefully slumbering in the passenger seat with her head resting against the window. Her long hair was tossed about over her face, and every so often she would let out a slight snore and attempt to reposition herself into a more comfortable position in the cramped front seat. *A far more attractive passenger than Krycerick.*

Jake braced himself as he carefully reached for the steering wheel with his left hand and brought his right hand down to the stick shift. He winced slightly as he did so. The engine roared with the car shifting into a lower gear as Jake exited the PCH and headed west on Dume Drive.

Brooke stirred. Her eyes opened and she raised her arms above her head in a big stretch, yawning as she did.

She combed her hair back off her face with her fingers and smiled at Jake shyly. "How long have I been out?"

Jake glanced down at the clock. *6:45.* "Almost three hours," he replied, as he again worked the stick and sped the car onto Cliffside Drive. He let out a groan.

"Oh, you poor thing," replied Brooke. She turned in her seat to face him. She looked concerned. "Is there anything I can do?"

Jake shook his head. "I'll be fine. We're almost at the house. You'll be safe there."

Brooke smiled. "I'm safe now," she replied, as she placed her hand softly on his shoulder. She let it linger for a moment, and when she got no reaction, she folded her hands in her lap. "You know, you saved all those people back at the hotel."

Jake turned to face her. He had only heard on the radio that the case was under investigation by the LVPD and that the hotel was refusing comment. "What have you heard?"

"Well, according to Mr. Shapiro . . ."

"Shapiro?" Jake interrupted, glancing over at Brooke.

"Yes," she replied. "He seems to know a lot about you. How do you think I found you at the hospital?"

Jake shook his head in amazement. "Terrific."

Brooke leaned over and kissed him on the cheek. "I knew I wouldn't be able to do that once we got to the house." She leaned back against the car door and brought her hand to her lips. She thought for a moment and then looked up at Jake. "Thank you, Jake."

"The hotel. What have you heard?"

Brooke sighed. "Everyone at The Palms got out safely." She paused. "You saved them. All of them." She paused again, this time longer. "Because of what you did no one was hurt." She frowned. "Except you, of course." She placed her hand back on Jake's shoulder. "Your wife is very lucky to have you, Jake."

Jake glanced down at his BlackBerry and shook his head. There was a litany of angry voice messages and e-mails all from Diane, and he knew she had every right to be pissed at him. "I'm not so sure she'd agree with you right about now," he muttered.

Once again the FBI had come between him and Diane. But was it the FBI, or was it him? *Good question.* It had been that way ever since he had been assigned to field work with his former boss, Ken Devasher. His assignments were extremely dangerous and always made Diane a nervous wreck. But Jake couldn't help it. He was addicted to it. He was an adrenaline junkie and he loved the rush. The more dangerous the mission, the better the high. But this time was different, and Jake knew it. It didn't matter if you were a lawyer working late preparing for a big trial or an FBI field agent getting blown across the room by C4 plastique. Never leave a pregnant wife stranded at the airport.

Jake brought the car to a stop in front of the gates at the bottom of the driveway and glanced at Brooke. "Look, when you meet my wife." He paused. "That whole explosion thing . . . well, let's just keep that between us, okay?"

Brooke shrugged. "Sure."

Jake rolled down the window and punched in a nine-digit security code. The gates slowly swung open and Jake sped up the driveway in the direction of the magnificent beach house, skidding to a halt on the gravel in front of the separate seven car garage.

Brooke's eyes widened. "Wow, this place is beautiful!"

Jake smiled, but stayed silent. He pressed a button on the dash and both car doors slowly glided open vertically, like an eagle raising its wings just before takeoff. He angled the rearview mirror toward him, looked closely at his face and ran his finger along the stitches above his eye. "Here we go," he mumbled to himself as he stepped out of the car and proceeded across the driveway to the front door.

Diane's father, the late Jack Sheppard, had purchased the 10,000 square foot estate that was nestled into one of the bluffs 100 feet above the Pacific Ocean a few years before his untimely death. It was a Spanish-style Mediterranean mansion with beige stucco walls, a deep orange terracotta roof and a multitude of balconies that hung over the jagged rocks facing the ocean.

"How much do you FBI guys make anyway?" asked Brooke, as she gazed around the magnificent landscaping and watched as a series of rugged waves crashed down onto the sand at the bottom of the bluff.

Jake reached into his pocket for his house keys, forgetting momentarily about his injured arm. The movement caused him to wince in pain as the keys dropped to the ground in front of the door. He closed his eyes and waited for the pain to subside. He took a deep breath, knelt down to retrieve the keys and looked up at Brooke. "Not nearly enough," he replied.

Just then the door to the house swung open. It was Diane. She had on a pair of grey sweats and a blue FBI T-shirt that accentuated her pregnancy. Her hair was tied back by a red bandana kerchief, and she was holding a Hershey bar in one hand and a jar of peanut butter in the other. She looked down at Jake who was still on his knees beside Brooke. "Really, Jake?" she said, in an annoyed tone.

Jake gave a nervous laugh. "Look Di Di, I can explain. There was this bomb . . ."

Diane held up her palm, cutting him off mid-sentence. She then looked over at Brooke, smiled politely, and extended her hand. "Hello, Ms. Sims. My name is Diane Chase."

Brooke returned the smile and the two women shook hands. "Very nice to meet you, Mrs. Chase."

Jake kept quiet and got back to his feet, smoothing out his clothes as he did so. Both women watched, amused, and then smiled at one another.

Diane gave a nod. "Can I interest you in a Hershey bar, Brooke?"

Brooke smiled. "I'd love one," she replied, as she walked past Jake and entered through the front door.

Once Brooke was inside the house Diane looked back at Jake, sternly at first, before her face melted into a sympathetic smile. "Are you okay, Jake?" she paused. "I love you so much and you know I hate it when you're in the field," she continued, with the sound of concern becoming present in her voice. She brought her hand to his face and gently ran her fingers along the tightly knit row of stitches. She shook her head. "Oh, Jake, do you ever actually win any of these fights?"

Jake grinned. "You should see the other guy," he replied, and then he leaned in and kissed her on the lips. When he pulled away he could see she looked worried. "Really, baby, I'm fine," he continued, but knew it would do no good to ease her frustration. "Look, LAPD will have this psycho under arrest soon and things will be back to normal, I promise."

Diane sighed and then wrapped her arms around him in a tight hug. "Jake, we need you," she whispered in his ear.

Jake's eyes widened as he gasped for air and struggled to control the pain that was now surging through his arm and shoulder. He could feel beads of sweat forming on his brow as he bit his lip to keep from screaming out in agony.

Diane kissed him on the cheek and squeezed herself even closer to him. "Please, Jake, be careful."

Jake fought to catch his breath and with all of the strength he could muster uttered the word, "Always."

CHAPTER 32

JAKE STRUGGLED BACK TO consciousness as he heard the sound of the French doors off the living room balcony slamming shut. His eyes then opened wide and he quickly sat up on the couch where he had passed out several hours before. Disoriented, he grabbed his gun from the coffee table, freed it from the leather shoulder harness and jumped to his feet. Instinctively, he scanned the large room with his gun clenched between his fists. *What now?* he thought, but then spotted Diane outside on the balcony relaxing on one of the chaise lounges. He let out a long sigh, shaking his head as he switched on the safety catch. "Fucking wind," he muttered, as he slid the Glock back into the shoulder holster and flung it onto the couch. "Get it together Jake, you're losing it man," he said, making his way across the room and out onto the balcony.

Diane looked up from her book and smiled. "Hey, have a good rest?"

Jake brought his hand to the back of his neck and tried to rub out some of the knots. His shoulder had stopped throbbing thanks to the codeine Diane had given him earlier. Having a wife who was also a doctor came in handy sometimes. He looked out over the stone railing and saw that the sun was starting to descend on the ocean. There was a cool breeze in the air and Jake watched as the rough tide slammed a volley of waves onto the rocky coast below. He yawned and turned to face Diane. "What time is it?" he asked, still a bit sluggish.

Diane set her book down on her lap and reached for her phone. She flipped it open and looked at the small screen. "6:15," she replied.

"Wow," replied Jake, as he took a seat next to her on a nearby lounge. "I've been out all day,"

Diane nodded. "Brooke, too. She's asleep in one of the guest rooms."

Jake reached for Diane's hand. "As soon as I hear from LAPD that they have this guy, she's gone, and we'll spend some quality time together, Di Di, I promise."

Diane smiled. "I've heard that one before." She then relaxed back into the chaise and re-opened her book.

"What are you reading?"

Diane looked at the book's hardcover and then angled it to face Jake. "It's a good book, Jake. You should read it. It's called, *What to Expect When You're Expecting.* I'll read you a few interesting points, you know, when we have this quality time you keep promising me." She smiled.

"I'd like that," replied Jake. "I really would." Then he leaned in and kissed her on the cheek. "I'm gonna go take a shower. Think about what you want to do for dinner," he said, as he walked through the French doors back into the living room. "I'm thinking Chinese."

Jake grabbed his BlackBerry from the table beside the couch and made his way through the master bedroom into the bathroom. He scrolled through his e-mails hoping for some positive news from Krycerick, but there was none. The only news was that they had found the killer's car abandoned in a parking lot just off the Vegas strip. "Wonderful," Jake muttered sarcastically as he powered off his BlackBerry. He opened the glass door to the shower and turned on the hot water full blast. The room quickly filled with steam as Jake carefully slid out of his shirt. The codeine was starting to wear off and his arm was beginning to ache again. The hot water would do him good. He was just about to unbutton his pants when he heard the distant sound of a door slamming. *Not again,* he thought. "Fuck it, probably just the ocean breeze," he said to his reflection in the foggy mirror, but then he hesitated. *What if it's not?* He reached into the shower, turned off the faucet and cautiously slipped out of the bathroom. He made his way down the long hallway in the direction of the living room. Suddenly, he heard a woman scream and the sound of glass shattering.

"Diane!" Jake shouted, charging down the hallway to the kitchen. As he ran through the door he saw a man standing over Brooke with a machete held high over his head. She was on her knees in front of him with her back to Jake. She was pleading with the man, her hands held in front of her face. The killer glanced up at Jake, but before he could react, Jake dove over Brooke's head and rammed his shoulder deep into the man's stomach like a linebacker bringing down the quarterback. The two men fell hard onto the stone floor with most of the weight landing on Jake's bad arm. Jake groaned as he brought his hand to his shoulder. The killer immediately seized the opportunity and forced Jake onto his back making sure to keep pressure on Jake's hurt arm. Quickly, he scrambled to retrieve the machete and brought it to

Jake's neck. He glanced over at Brooke, who had been knocked out in the scuffle.

"Hello, Deputy Director," said the killer sarcastically as he pressed the blade of the machete tightly against Jake's neck. "My name is Burns Newman and you and Ms. Sims over there are gonna make me famous." He grinned sadistically. "What do you think of that, superstar?"

Jake clenched his teeth tightly. He could feel blood trickling down his neck from where the blade was cutting into him and his arm was now throbbing with pain. "Fuck you, asshole!"

For a moment the killer appeared stunned. Then he smiled. "A tough guy right to the end." He took a deep breath and exhaled through his nose. "Well, I'll make sure you get credit for that in the movie." He then forced his hand down tightly on Jake's shoulder and was about to raise the blade above his head when suddenly something soared over Jake's head and hit the killer on the bridge of his nose. It stunned the man for a moment, but a moment was all Jake needed. Instantly, Jake freed his arms, grabbed the killer's hands and forced the machete to swing down hard straight into the killer's heart. His eyes rolled into the back of his head and he fell to the ground.

Jake screamed and jumped to his feet. He turned to face the door and there was Diane. She was leaning against the wall, pale with shock. Slowly, she slid her back down the wall until she was in a sitting position. She placed her hands on her tummy. "This can't be good for the babies."

Jake looked down at the killer lying dead on the floor. Next to him was Diane's book, *What to Expect When You're Expecting*. "That is a good book," Jake muttered.

He then turned back to Diane. "Are you okay?" he asked, kneeling beside her.

"Oh, ya know, a little heartburn, always have to pee. The usual when you're six months pregnant."

Jake heard the sound of police sirens approaching the house.

Diane held up her cell phone. "Not that I don't have the utmost confidence in you, Jake," Diane said with a slight smile.

"What happened? Is everyone okay?" asked Brooke as she slowly made her way to her feet. Then she noticed the killer's body and let out a yelp. "Oh my God, is that him?" she asked, backing up to the door. "How did he find us?"

Jake stood and helped Diane to her feet. The sirens were getting closer. "Yes, that's him, he's dead. It's all over." said Jake. Then a quizzical look came over his face. He thought for a minute and looked at Diane, confused. He leaned into her and took a whiff. "Are you wearing perfume?"

"Have you lost your mind, Jake?"

"Perfume, the kind I buy you. You know, Caron's Poivre. Are you wearing it now?"

"No, Jake," replied Diane, shaking her head. "I'm not wearing any perfume."

He then turned to Brooke. "You?"

Brooke shrugged. "No, Jake, I'm not."

Jake brought his palms to his face. "It's on my hands. I can smell it," he said, looking around the room, confused. Then it occurred to him. He froze as suddenly it all made sense. "She was in on it the whole time. That's where he was getting his information. That's how he knew where everyone was."

"Who?" asked Diane.

Jake walked up to the killer's body and knelt beside him. He leaned in and inhaled deeply. "Caron's Poivre. I recognized that smell the first day I met her." He shook his head. "It's very unique."

"Who?" asked Diane and Brooke in unison.

"Tyler Paige," replied Jake.

CHAPTER 33

JAKE COULD SEE THE CITY LIGHTS come into view as the chopper soared through the night sky in the direction of LAX. He knew that with rush hour traffic it could take hours to get to Los Angeles, regardless of how fast he drove Brooke's Lamborghini, so he decided to call in a favor from his new pal, Korean War vet Chuck Parker.

Jarvis had run a search on David Kossow, the lawyer whose business card Jake had found in the killer's pocket. After a brief interrogation by some local FBI field men, Kossow copped a deal and confessed to everything. *Fucking lawyers.*

Apparently, he and Tyler Paige had been lovers for years, and they had planned the string of brutal Hollywood murders several months after Paramount. Tyler had met Burns Newman at a party and knew instantly that she could manipulate him into doing anything she wanted, especially with his hatred for Lefty Shapiro. After all, Lefty had ruined his life. With a little help from her girlfriend at the pharmacy, keeping old Burnsie heavily medicated was a cinch. After a brief interview with Lefty, she was hired by the agency and the wheels were in motion.

"The private aviation hangars are on the North side of the airport," yelled Chuck into the microphone on his headset. He pointed off into the distance where

233

long rows of white lights illuminated several runways. "Hangar 15, right?"

Jake nodded. "Yeah, 15."

Kossow had arranged for a private jet to fly him and Tyler down to Mexico for a few weeks. After all, what could be better than sipping margaritas on the beach in Acapulco, while putting the finishing touches on the perfectly executed plan?

"Okay, Jake," said Chuck, as he brought the chopper down about a hundred yards from hangar 15. "Sure you don't need any backup?"

Jake smiled and extended his hand. "Thanks, Chuck. I got this."

The two men shook hands and Jake jumped out of the chopper and made his way across the dark runway in the direction of the hangar. He knew he had to be on his A-game so he had decided it was best to lay off the codeine. Instead, Diane had taped his arm and shoulder, and, all things considered, the pain seemed tolerable—especially with the adrenaline rushing through his veins.

As he approached the hangar, he took out his Glock, gripped it tightly between both hands and held it close to his chest. Cautiously, he entered the brightly lit room through a small opening in the large steel doors. He immediately spotted Tyler and ducked behind a long row of shelving. She was standing next to the jet and was saying something to the pilot. She was dressed in a tight-fitting skirt, a halter top and black leather boots that came up to her knees. With her hair teased wildly off her face, Jake almost didn't recognize her as the same woman he had met at the Shapiro Agency.

The pilot nodded and made his way up the hatch into the plane.

Tyler looked at her watch and shook her head. She turned to face the hangar doors and muttered something under her breath about lawyers never being on time. She then reached into her purse, took out a cigarette and placed it between her lips. As she reached back in for her lighter, Jake stepped out from behind the shelving with his gun still clenched between both fists, now pointing at her head.

"Need a light?" asked Jake, sarcastically. Then he grinned and started walking toward her with his gun leading the way.

Tyler looked at him and her shoulders dropped. "Jesus Christ!" she exclaimed. "I mean really, can't you just die?"

Jake kept his gun pointed at her head and continued in her direction. "Tyler Paige, you are under arrest for conspiracy in the murders of Skyler Dawn, Trevor Hash and Jesse James."

With her hand still inside her purse, Tyler let go of her cigarette lighter and gripped a small nickel-plated revolver, placed her finger on the trigger and angled it in Jake's direction. She smiled at him seductively. "I don't suppose I can interest you in making a deal, huh Jake?"

Jake stayed silent.

Tyler frowned. "I didn't think so," she said and was just about to squeeze the trigger when a loud gunshot echoed through the cavernous hangar. BANG!

The noise startled Jake; he felt something whiz past his head, missing his ear by inches. Quickly, he turned to face the hangar doors and saw Krycerick, grinning as he blew the smoke from his gun's barrel. His eyes widened as he turned back to see Tyler, who had a look of horror on her face. Her purse dropped to the ground revealing to Jake the small pistol she had been concealing. Tyler let out a slight gasp as she looked down at the small hole in her halter-top. Her shirt turned a dark shade of red as she dropped to her knees. She looked up at Jake one last time and then fell; face first, onto the concrete floor.

Jake let out a huff as he lowered the gun in front of him. He brought his hand to his ear to make sure the bullet had clipped no part of it.

Krycerick walked up to Jake and placed his hand on his shoulder. He looked down at Tyler's body and shook his head. "Chicks."

Jake nodded. "Yup." Then he turned to face Krycerick. "Nice shot, Nails. But do you think you could have gotten it any closer to my head?"

Krycerick let out a cackle. "That bullet missed ya by a mile."

Jake brought his hand back to his ear. He holstered his gun and started walking toward the hangar doors. "Come on, let's get the fuck out of here. I'll buy you a chocolate milk."

Krycerick smiled. "You're on, Deputy Director."

"You ever think of coming to work for the Feds, Nails?" asked Jake, as he approached the opening in the doors.

"FBI Agent Nails Krycerick. I kinda like the sound of that."

Jake let Krycerick pass through the doors first. He turned back and looked down at Tyler's body lying in a pool of her own blood at the foot of the Gulfstream jet. He let out a humble sigh as he brought his hand to his shoulder. He winced. The adrenaline was wearing off and the pain was quickly coming back. He shook his head. "I can't believe I'm back in fucking LA!"

THE END